Clockmaker's
Christmas

BOOKS BY SHIRLEY BURTON

THRILLERS

UNDER THE ASHES
Book One of the Thomas York Series
THE FRIZON
Book Two of the Thomas York Series
ROGUE COURIER
Book Three of the Thomas York Series
SECRET CACHE
Book Four of the Thomas York Series
RED JACKAL

MYSTERY
SENTINEL IN THE MOORS

HISTORICAL FICTION
HOMAGE: CHRONICLES OF A HABITANT

CHRISTMAS
CLOCKMAKER'S CHRISTMAS

shirleyburtonbooks.com

Clockmaker's Christmas

Shirley Burton

HIGH STREET PRESS

CALGARY

HIGH STREET PRESS
Calgary, AB
highstreetpress.com
shirleyburtonbooks.com
First printing 2017

Printed in the United States of America and worldwide under license.
Available in eBook formats.
Design and editing Bruce Burton
Cover Bruce Burton, photo licensed Shutterstock.com.

Burton, Shirley, 1950-, author
        Clockmaker's christmas / Shirley Burton

Issued in print and electronic versions.
ISBN 978-1-927839-12-6 (pbk.). —ISBN 978-1-927839-13-3 (hardcover)
ISBN 978-1-927839-14-0 (ebook)

He looked through the curtains to a full moon. Somewhere beyond, he was sharing the same moon with Rosa, and he repeated the words in his head of the nostalgic wartime song by Billy Holiday, I'll be Seeing You.

1

Rosa batted a snowflake on her cheek as she emerged from the subway steps into a mob of festive shoppers.

At the curb at 34th and Broadway, a plow dumped a load of slush at her feet as she set to cross. With arms stretched, she took two brave strides into the wet snowbank, aware it would soak over the tops of her fur-lined galoshes. Others at the stoplight watched her feet and quickly followed in her tracks.

The night sky had descended, and the streets and sidewalks of New York glistened in the reflection of neon lights. Rosa paused in front of Macy's to take in the chatter of Christmas revelers, and nodded at innocent faces pressed to the glass and glued to the magic of the animations.

Evening shifts at the glove counter always rewarded her, but never more than this season in the weeks of December, when the store became a visual fantasyland.

Elmer Harris stood in a Santa suit on one leg outside the store, ringing a Sally Ann bell for kettle donations. His missing leg was left back at Vimy Ridge, and he propped up his balance with a wooden contraption.

Elmer played the part perfectly, jolly and with a natural, bushy white beard. Seeing him again, Rosa was reminded of heroic veterans from World War II and the Korean War, many that struggled to integrate again into an everyday life.

"Good evening, Mr. Harris. It's gratifying to see you each day."

Rosa was prepared with only a dime from her milk and bread fund from over the stove back home. She listened as it jingled deep into the pot of coins. Elmer had reminded her more than once that it was a ball of hope and benevolence.

"Merry Christmas! God Bless, Rosa," he called, knowing her first name like others from the store.

Elmer's bell chimed again as she moved on, and his 'Ho-Ho-Ho's were soon drowned by a background of Victorian-attired carolers. Rosa could still hear strains of his cheery greetings as she neared the entrance.

Businesses were closing for the day as Manhattan's skyscrapers emptied employees into the streets and subways, women with stylish coats and handbags, and men with gray fedoras and leather briefcases. As a bus unloaded a crowd from the suburbs, she blended into the genial throng and squeezed with them through Macy's giant revolving glass door.

At the bank of elevators, she waited in a queue for her turn, and as the brass gate opened, a uniformed man with braided epaulets and a shiny brimmed hat called to her from a stool inside the carriage. "C'mon Rosa, I've got room for one more."

She tightened in past the others, close enough to talk. "Good evening, Harold."

"Is it still Christmas outside?" the old man teased.

"Of course, Harold. It will be Christmas as long as Macy's says so."

"I 'spose you're right. All the stores are open late 'til Christmas to give us working folks a chance to shop. Ads in the Times say Gimbels and Bergdorf's are following suit. Saturday night I'll be off to shop, and then the grandkids are in a concert Sunday at St. Mary's."

"These are truly the best times, Harold."

The elevator bars folded closed like an accordion with the touch of his handle. On the third floor, Rosa inched to the exit. "Enjoy your little ones this weekend," she whispered.

She eyed the clock over the elevator—4:55. With only minutes at hand, she wasted no time in the staff cloakroom, punching her time card, and storing her coat, felt hat and galoshes.

Passing the elevator again, Rosa screeched to a stop to refresh her lipstick in the mirrored plate, and flipped back her locks. In a final dash, she slipped on one foot as she reached the counter, and Iris caught her elbow.

"Doesn't pay Rosa to run."

"Sorry I'm late."

"Naw, Rosa. It's 5:02 p.m. by Mr. Macy's time, but don't give it a thought. How are your boys today?"

"Thanks, Iris. You never have a harsh word. Edgar arrived from school when I was about to leave . . . another fresh bruise on his cheek. Will was silent as ever and went to his room. It's hard being a single parent, leaving a hot meal on the table and walking out the door. I knew Edgar wanted to talk, but I'd be late for my train."

"I'm so sorry, Rosa, but feeling guilty isn't good for you."

"I've been fighting with the Veterans department to get Jake's pension started, but it's been a brick wall. They have yet to determine if Jake was killed by enemy fire or engine failure . . . or heaven forbid, what they call 'friendly fire'. The sad part is that I'm not the only widow living in limbo.

"Let's keep our fingers crossed." Iris smiled warmly. "Do you need a lawyer?"

"I have an appointment at their New Jersey office next week. I can't afford a lawyer. But you met my cousin Vivian Watson . . . her husband Lloyd was a court clerk and she thinks he can give me advice."

Within minutes of opening, two male customers arrived for help, drawing both Rosa and Iris out to the sales floor, one for a silk scarf and the other gloves.

"Come with me, Mr. Rutherford," Rosa said. "I know you'll find our glove selection suitable for both your wife and mother."

Rutherford picked two pairs, a navy wrist-length with sweet pearl buttons at the cuff, and long, black sleek gloves almost to the elbow. It was clear to Rosa which was for the wife. She boxed each with a fine tissue and a glossy white box crested with Macy's logo.

"Mr. Rutherford, if you can shop for a bit, I'll have these wrapped. They'll be ready in an hour."

With a burden lifted, Mr. Rutherford poured out his relief and thanks, and ventured deep into the store. Rosa flipped on the red light over her counter to alert Henry from Gift Wrap that she had a pickup.

"Iris, I couldn't work anywhere else," Rosa confessed. "This man just told me I've made his own family's Christmas morning better."

"You're making me feel responsible for other's happiness," Iris laughed. Rosa's eyes flashed to the thought of her boys and the delight they'll show with the modest gifts she could afford.

Since the Thanksgiving Parade, Macy's Herald Square Christmas displays had been the season's biggest attraction for New Yorkers, with families lined at the windows, the youngest ones mesmerized at mechanics of the moving display. It was a tradition with Rosa's own two boys that before seeing Santa inside, their faces would press to the frosty glass outside, watching the electric trains that delivered parcels in one window, and the animated toy workshop in the next.

Inside, store carols replayed in sequence, and when Bing Crosby finally crooned *White Christmas* for the sixth time that evening, Rosa knew it was close to store closing.

"Get home to your boys, Rosa. Sign off on the sales sheet and I'll take the pouch to the office. You don't want to miss the 9:40 p.m."

"You're an angel. Have I said that before?"

At the cloak room, her thoughts sped faster.

The boys will be in bed. I wonder if they did their homework. I forgot to reply to Vivian about Christmas dinner. It is kind of her to look out for us since Jake went missing. I'm getting stronger every day— I must for our boys.

She hardly remembered the next hour, walking in the same routine to the subway, riding to Grand Central, and crossing the Queensboro Bridge on the rush hour express. At her brownstone, off 39th in Queens, she opened the wrought iron gate and looked up to see Edgar's face in the upstairs parlor window, leaning at the frosted pane, watching for her.

Something's wrong.

At the door she greeted and excused Mrs. Fitch, her neighbor who minded them after school. Rushing up, she met Edgar in the hall with his door partially open.

"Edgar, what is it? Has something happened? You should have gone to bed an hour ago."

"Yes, Mom. But I think something important has come for you, and my curiosity wouldn't let me sleep. It's in the kitchen and I'll get it. Will is sound asleep though with the sleep fairies." He beamed, "And I washed all the dishes and swept the floor."

Rosa was anxious undoing her galoshes, and draped her coat over a kitchen chair.

"Here, Mom. A man delivered this from the telegraph office. He said it came all the way from Germany for you."

Edgar sat down beside his mother, and for a moment seemed older to her.

"Hmm . . . thin airmail onion skin . . . Edgar, can you please bring the letter opener from the hall bureau.

With one swipe, the brass blade split open the crease. "The stamps are beautiful, would you like them for your collection?"

"Yes, please."

She read the brief words silently, then out loud for Edgar's curious ears.

RE ESTATE OF HERR ABEL BRAND.
IMPORTANT TO CONTACT MR. ARMBRUSTER

A long distance phone number was at the bottom, and the signature of a Berlin barrister from an office in Heidelberg.

"Well, bless my boots, Edgar. I haven't heard that name since your Dad and I were first married."

"Who is Herr Brand?"

"It's a long story, but for now you must get off to bed. Did you both get your homework done?"

Edgar didn't budge.

"Yes Mom. Are you sure you don't want to talk?"

Rosa looked down at Edgar, now seven and the image of his father, with strawberry blond hair and twinkling green eyes.

Gently, her finger ran over the darkening bruise on his cheek. "And what is this? Was it absolutely necessary, Edgar?"

"A few boys were picking on Will, so I did what I had to. Don't worry, the other kid didn't get hurt and Will is fine. A gang of school bullies get a kick out of torturing little boys."

Edgar hesitated and looked into Rosa's eyes as she waited for more.

"Then Butch McGinnis said our Dad was a coward and ran away from the war. I couldn't let him away with that."

"You are wiser than your years, Edgar. Thanks for looking out for Will. But if I need to talk to the principal at school, you'll let me know?"

"We'll be fine, Mom. You don't need to worry about me."

Rosa tousled his hair and dispatched him down the hall to the bedroom he shared with young Will, but a concerned pain stabbed her in the heart.

He shouldn't have to go through this—Jake is a hero.

With Edgar tucked in, Rosa searched the back of the bureau drawer for a packet of envelopes tied with kitchen twine, each with the rugged scrawl of Jacob Stanford.

On the Marconi turntable, she lowered the needle to play the family's Christmas LP of Gene Autry's *Rudolph the Red-Nosed Reindeer*, then went to the window to pull back the lace curtains. The huge flakes were drifting to the ground, with the street becoming a white blanket with the shimmering glow of moonlight and its long shadows.

By the parlor window, she snuggled into her favorite overstuffed armchair, the one where Jake used to sit with his newspaper in the evenings after dinner. She went back to thumb through the envelopes, her mind on the name Brand.

2

March 1959, Ramstein Air Base, Germany

Jacob George Stanford had grown up in the Bavarian village of Heidelberg, east of the French border on the Neckar River, in the state of Baden-Württemberg. He left his homeland before WWII to live in the States, and first served in front line battle during the Korean War. A scar on his cheek the length of his temple to the bottom of his ear was a souvenir of an old shrapnel wound.

In 1958, Jake was recalled to serve in Germany, where the U.S. air bases reinforced French and West German troops against invasion from communists in Czechoslovakia. At the onset of the Cold War, he enlisted in the 86th Wing of the U.S. Air Force, at an air base in the Rhine Valley that served the 7030th combat support battalion.

As Americans performed reconnaissance over Germany, their training missions often wandered near or into Soviet air space, with the enemy responding by randomly shooting down Allied planes over the Black Sea and the Baltic. Tragically, from 1950 to 59, more than 19 planes had been downed by 23 mm fire from Russian MiG aircraft.

Many crew members were killed taking fire from the Soviets, but those that survived and landed in enemy territory were less lucky. More than half were murdered in interrogation, with many tortured; others died in prisons without the American government knowing of their status.

Jake Stanford's knowledge of German was helpful, and he joined others in the rescue of refugees on helicopter manoeuvers near Brandenburg, and was selected for elite missions with experimental aircraft. In 1958, Soviet Premier Khrushchev demanded that U.S., British and French troops withdraw from Germany, and debates soared over the building of the Berlin wall.

In New York, Jake had left behind his young bride of five years and their two sons, Edgar at four back then and Will in her arms. A well-thumbed photo of his family never left him, and was always in his shirt pocket, folded flat for platoon inspection. At five eleven and 175 pounds, he used to tease Rosa that he was nondescript, with light golden brown hair, shorn into a crew cut.

Frequently, Jake was paired with the same co-pilot, Vince Moretti, and usually was joined in the turret bubble under the nose by Weasel, their gunner, or sometimes Jan Huffman. The space for a shooter was cramped, requiring a small stature of less than five nine, ideal for Weasel or Jan.

During their last two years of duty together, Jake and Moretti became close, facing and surviving too many life and death scrapes, as the unit was deployed to Allied bases. Many times, his friends and teammates were replaced, from reassignments or losses in battle.

"Time for a bite, Jake," Moretti called into the tent. "Hey, are you sleeping? I picked up tomorrow's assignment and it's a doozy."

Jake raised his head from the cot.

"Not sleeping at all. I'm writing to Rosa in New York. And what's the doozy . . . good or bad?"

"Big, that's all I know. We ship out early for training exercises on the phantom DR 152 over Ottendorf-Okrilla. Last week was its successful maiden flight, and we are the goats now."

"Ottendorf! Blessed Mary!"

"Exactly my thought. The airspace is thick with Soviet MiGs waiting for an excuse to fire on an American plane. If we dared to stray over Prague, we'd been downed mercilessly."

"What is the mission?"

"A test run with photos of the Russian convoy and land movement of their troops."

"A spy mission," Jake said.

Moretti nodded. "Innocent Czechs are forced to wave the swastika and even fire on their own. Every few nights, the midnight patrol finds escapees from Prague crawling under barbed wire and through muddy ditches in the darkness. Last night a young girl with a sick baby barely made it out."

"She must have left a family behind too." Jake breathed deeply and returned the photo of Rosa and the boys to his pocket. With his hand pressed to it, he bounded off the bed, stuffed his essentials into a burlap sack and lined up his boots to polish.

"Leave that, Jake, and we'll go to the mess tent for coffee and something warm. It's blustery out there so get a coat for the wind."

The sky was dark under clouds with wet blowing snow. Jake plucked his heavy camouflage jacket from its hook and sealed the door securely.

Behind a dozen others, Jake and Moretti inched the trays down the line, all of them hoping for anything hot. Jake spotted Weasel up in front.

"Hey pal, I heard we'll be joining you in the morning."

Weasel was soft-spoken, with an earned and often comical reputation for wiggling into cramped planes to manage the turret guns. His heroics had led to a victory over the Koreans when he smuggled dynamite into an enemy foxhole and squirmed back under the thorny wire to safety before it was detonated.

"The weather report for tomorrow is even worse than tonight," Weasel said. "Today I was up before daybreak and barely made it back to base through the blizzard. The Soviet MiGs are enjoying the cloud cover, but thank goodness for our radar. Say your prayers tonight, boys!"

The night wind howled through the tented village, drifting waves of snow across the compound.

Jake was slipping into a light sleep at midnight when the air raid sirens blared across the base. Donning his boots, he ran with his jacket open to line up for formation.

The commander shouted into a megaphone, but his words were whipped into the wind. "Men, already a squadron of MiGs is circling into our airspace. Last night, we caught a Czech soldier tunneling under the wire. He asked for asylum and gave us credible information to a planned pre-dawn ambush. Take your positions with your aircraft, and we'll move them to a safe base near Munich under camouflage. If we do get bombed, our planes will be spared."

With limited lighting they moved quickly, knowing the attack could be imminent, and at 4:10 a.m. their flight tower detected movement north of Prague entering German airspace.

"Stanford and Moretti! Take Baade DR-152 unit Zebra and fly the border tracking their convoy. Don't fire unless you are fired upon. Understand?"

"Yes, Captain." Stanford saluted and stood at attention for the last time on duty.

Two hours later, a scrambled Mayday message from Zebra said they'd been hit by Russian missile fire. An accompanying fighter jet reported there'd been at least one ejection as the plane spiraled down into the hills, followed by a catastrophic burst of flames.

Hours later, a chopper with a search crew found the wreckage inside the German border without any sign of the victims. A singed picture of Rosa and the boys was tucked into a slot against the windshield.

As a barrage of Soviet tanks rolled towards them, the rescue chopper took fire as it lifted off to Ramstein, returning safely but empty-handed.

3

December 3, 1962, Borough of Queens, New York

*R*osa rifled into the letter bundle, searching her memory for something to connect to Abel Brand.

"Sometime in February 1958."

She held a crumpled envelope to the light. The sight of Jake's handwriting caused her eyes to well, and her fingers trembled. "This is it, I'm sure."

> *My darling Rosa,*
>
> *I long for the day when I can hold you in my arms again. I will be up for furlough in a few months.*
>
> *Last week, I took Moretti with me for a few days leave. We spent two nights in charming Heidelberg. The town took a beating in the 40's but is now struggling to rebuild.*
>
> *On a lark, I asked at the market by the old bridge if my mother's father still lived nearby. I'd forgotten the house, but I*

remembered the outside of the building from pictures my mother had. I still think of her every Christmas Eve. You know her name was Eve. She married my father, George Stanford, in the 30's and I don't remember her mentioning him much after that. Her own father was Abel Brand.

I couldn't believe my eyes when I stood in front of Bachmann's Bavarian Clocks, which was the business under my grandparents' apartment. Old Mr. Bachmann told me that Grandad was still living. Although in failing health, he was spunky as ever.

I'm afraid I startled Grandad rather badly, but he knew me right away. He said I have my mother's eyes and the same freckles across my nose. I took it as a great compliment.

After a grand visit, we walked over the Neckar Bridge then on the boardwalk below. He talked of the fear they lived in during the Great War, having to carry papers wherever they went. He stopped at a spot by the river bank where the bricks were crumbling. He said it was used by fleeing Germans to communicate with relatives and friends, without the Soviets knowing.

I promised to bring my family back someday soon when the world will be at peace again. Perhaps you could tell the boys that they have kinfolk here in Germany.

I promise to be home soon.

Love you always. Jake

With her finger to her lips, Rosa placed a kiss on the letter. As the envelope flittered to her lap, her thoughts wandered and she looked out to the dark sky.

"They never found a body and the Soviets didn't give up his name among their prisoners. In these three years, I am still waiting to grieve, yet I am ashamed to live in a country of peace while Jake could be alive in a terrible prison, or worse."

Laying on the double bed, she wrapped her arms around Jake's pillow and sobbed into sleep.

Edgar poked his head into the kitchen. "Mornin' Mom. What's for breakfast?"

"Did you sleep well, Darlin'?"

"Better than you," Edgar smirked. Down the hall the toilet flushed and Rosa knew that Will was up too.

"Why do you say that, Edgar?"

"I got up to use the bathroom in the night and the house was dark, except a light under your door. Is it something to do with Herr Brand?"

Pain crossed Rosa's face and she recovered quickly. "Not exactly. We'll talk later when you're home from school. I was missing your Dad. I'm so glad I have my boys. Always know how much you are loved. Together, the three of us will keep each other strong."

Rosa doled scoops into their three bowls, and called into the narrow hall. "Will—it's time for breakfast. Red River, your favorite."

In Davy Crockett flannel PJs, Will arrived to his mother's lap, propping his head to her shoulder. "Not porridge today, Mom. It's my tummy."

Rosa touched his forehead. "I'll arrange for Mrs. Fitch to watch you. Off with you now, back to bed."

The bus honked below on the street, and Rosa admired Edgar's blonde curls as he skipped downstairs with his Rin Tin lunch box.

"Love you, Mom," he called as the door clicked.

There was still time to phone her cousin Vivian about Christmas dinner. "Of course, the boys will be with me . . . and my famous glazed apple turnip casserole and a layered jelly mold, if you can stand that for a third year in a row."

Vivian was the daughter of Rosa's mother's sister, and the cousins grew up close like siblings. Vivian's husband, Lloyd, had prospered in his cement business and the family had afforded a house in an affluent district close to Manhattan.

Thank goodness for Vivian. What would I do without her?

Rosa marked it on the calendar beside the refrigerator. She'd been scheduled to work Christmas Eve but had traded with Iris for the day shift. Every year since Rosa and Jake were married, they went to St. Mary's Nativity pageant, and she now vowed to never miss the event and the memory it spurred.

Will made it to the couch to sleep, and Rosa tucked an afghan over him. She kissed his forehead, then set the kettle on the burner to heat up for Mrs. Fitch. With only three weeks to Christmas, she was burdened with how the call to Germany might change her life.

I'll leave it one more day. Iris will have suggestions for me.

It was payday and she'd make another weekly layaway payment at the store. With two more installments, they'd go to Gift Wrap. She was certain of her choices from the well-thumbed Macy's catalogue—Edgar left a neat fold on the page corner for the electric train, and Will was bolder, turning the entire page of the Meccano set halfway to the spine.

In minutes, Mrs. Fitch arrived, coming the few steps from the end of the hall. "Mrs. Fitch, thanks so much. The kettle just whistled for your morning tea, but I must leave to make it by 10."

"Of course, Rosa . . . you be off. And poor laddie Will. I'll turn on the Christmas radio plays for the two of us and then knit up a storm."

"He'll pester you for Roy Rogers and Dale Evans on TV, or the Lone Ranger; and he likes Woody Woodpecker at noon. But don't let him sit close to the screen."

"No worry, Rosa, I remember how boys think. We'll have a grand time."

"He hasn't eaten, but Campbell's Chicken noodle soup and saltines are on the counter. If he gets his appetite, he can have graham wafers and tapioca pudding."

Mrs. Fitch listened patiently and nodded convincingly, but Rosa hesitated and they both smirked to acknowledge that her instructions were apt to change. Raising her own children and grandchildren taught Mrs. Fitch that the best lure to get them off the couch would be home-baked cookies and warm banana bread.

Mildred Fitch was a stately woman, tall and slender, with a magnificent bouffant of a grey upsweep and milky porcelain skin, always leaving the aroma of Lily of the Valley. Rosa figured she must have been a real beauty in her day.

"What would I do without you, Mildred?"

At the Lexington subway station, she transferred on 59th Avenue and disembarked at Broadway. In a hurried pace to Macy's, she slid through the slushy curb, and slowed only enough to drop today's dime into Elmer's kettle.

With a bustle of the crowd congregating for the store to open, she realised seconds too late that it was her transit token that clinked to the bottom. Elmer roared his delight at her mistake, and curious shoppers turned their heads at the volume of his belly laugh and to watch his antics.

"No issue to fish it out, Rosa. Consider it a pleasure for the extra moment."

At the locker, Rosa turned her boot cuffs back and inverted them under her bench. Warm air was flowing from the baseboard heater and she hoped her galoshes would be warm and dry before her shift ended at six.

At her station, Iris was polishing the glass counter tops, and Rosa reached for the rag to take over. "Patience Iris, it's my turn," she teased. "Couldn't you wait two minutes?"

Iris relinquished the soft cloth. "Sorry, sweetie. You know how I am about greasy handprints on the glass. These pricy gloves would be ruined if stained."

"Will is home sick today. I'm so blessed to have Mildred Fitch down the hall. She's like a grandmother to the boys."

"You're lucky, Rosa. My girls are old enough to stay on their own, but I remember days of trying to find a reliable sitter."

As Macy's front doors opened, the P.A. began the announcements of early store specials in the Toy department and Ladies lingerie. The rush of shoppers would take minutes more to reach the accessories section on the second floor, and Rosa took the moments to confide in Iris.

"When I got home last night, a telegram was waiting—from Germany. I need to phone a lawyer there about an estate from Jake's maternal grandfather." She lightened it with a laugh, "And I don't even know how to make a transatlantic call. Do you?"

"My Mom is in London," Iris said. "I call at Christmas and her birthday and never talk long as it gets expensive. Dial zero and ask for the German exchange, and th operator will ring the number. If it's busy, they call back. It's about six hours' time change, so early morning should get through."

"I can handle that. I'll have to deal with this soon—Jake would want me to."

"Do you know the grandfather's situation?"

"Not really. I went through Jake's letters and he mentioned a leave to Heidelberg a few months before he disappeared. He tracked his grandfather that lives over a clock store."

"Heidelberg sounds exotic. Isn't it where Heidi the mountain girl lived? I remember reading one of the Whitman books. It was either the Black Forest or the Swiss Alps." They both laughed.

"Me too. As a girl, I loved the fantasy of books and always read myself to sleep. Last night, I thumbed through a box of Jake's family pictures. In one, an older couple was standing in front of a cuckoo shop with a castle as the background. A shadow of a man behind gave me the chills; he was so familiar that I thought for a moment it was Jake."

"Now Rosa, that's fantasy and not common sense," Iris said with concern.

"Right you are. Here come some shoppers."

Back at the brownstone, Rosa wondered what time it would be in Germany.

Would Herr Armbruster be in his office?

With the advice from Iris, Rosa placed the transatlantic call to the lawyer's office early the next morning. After a minute of static, the line clicked and a heavy voice answered.

"Herr Armbruster?"

"Yes, this must be Madame Stanford. I'm glad you called. I'll be to the point. It is important that you come to Heidelberg as soon as possible. Herr Brand owned an apartment building and we are deluged with applicants wanting to let. Also, there is an offer on the cuckoo shop where he was a full partner. If we don't take care of this quickly, squatter's rights will apply and it will take years in court."

"I'm afraid I know so little about Abel Brand."

"We have information that your husband, Jacob George Stanford, was the only heir."

"Yes?" Rosa said, after difficulty clearing her throat.

"We placed the required legal notice in our newspapers for a three week bann and no one came forward to object. The will stipulates that if Jacob does not survive his grandfather, the estate goes to his next of kin. That would be you, Mrs. Stanford."

Rosa reached for a chair, and her hesitation prodded him to continue. "The estate is substantial. We are in a position to send a prepaid ticket for you to come."

"I have small children, Mr. Armbruster."

"See what you can arrange. In the meantime, I'll advance an open ticket for you to the Lufthansa office at Idlewild Airport."

Still numb, Rosa covered her eyes with her hand. "I'll let you know what I can arrange."

Half an hour later, she called again.

"Mr. Armbruster, you don't understand my position. I am a widow with two young children. I depend on my weekly pay cheek to provide food and shelter. I'm not in a financial situation to travel."

"No problem, Mrs. Stanford. Give me your banking details and we'll wire a $500 U.S. travel advance to your bank. Will that be sufficient?"

"Yes, thank you. I have an account at Marine Midland Bank on 34th Avenue in Manhattan. I'll need a few days to make arrangements." Rosa couldn't believe the calm authority in her voice and the decisiveness she'd projected.

"If you are able, Mrs. Stanford, come directly and you'll be back home for Christmas."

"Then I'll plan to travel Tuesday and I'll telegram details."

Off the call, Rosa checked her calendar. Tomorrow would be Saturday and she was double-shifted, then Sunday she'd take the boys to Church. With a flurry of calls to Vivian and Mrs. Fitch, she was assured that the boys would be well fussed over.

The advance came instantly as promised and she felt a burden eased.

Tomorrow between shifts, I'll look for new winter boots with my staff discount. And the boys can shop with me after work at Piggly Wiggly.

A call to Macy's confirmed what she knew, that family comes first, and a guarantee that her position would be waiting for her return from Germany.

In a New Testament packed in the Pullman for clothes, Rosa placed a photo of the couple at the cuckoo shop, one of Jake, and school pictures of the boys. On Saturday night, she placed the case beside the door, with a portable train case of toiletries.

4

Flight New York to Heidelberg

In the dark hours of Monday morning, Rosa kissed her groggy boys and scurried to the waiting cab, indulging with taxi fare to LaGuardia.

Lufthansa had called in the evening that her ticket was waiting. She double checked her handbag for her passport, and felt inside her wallet for the hand-printed note of next of kin and contacts for her New York family.

Rosa had never traveled outside of the United States. One cold winter before Jake was called for his third tour of duty, they had driven to Florida but she'd never been on a jetliner, let alone crossing the Atlantic.

The airport was in a third renovation and was touted in the news as a beacon of industrial design. She was glad she hadn't taken a shuttle with the confusion and commotion of the construction. A cluster of redcap porters stood curbside to assist with luggage in exchange for a reasonable tip. Rosa had no time to object when a porter in full uniform lifted her bags to a dolly, and escorted her to Lufthansa's desk.

She dug into her change purse. "Thank you, Sir. I can manage from here."

The check-in clerk wore a smart uniform with a perky teal hat, and Rosa examined the woman's red and blue scarf, contemplating whether it might be a nylon fabric, now more commonly replacing silk.

"Can I help you, Ma'am?" She looked up from the scarf.

"Rosa Stanford. A prepaid ticket should be here for me."

The clerk ran her fingers through a wooden index box. "Ah, here we are. And may I see your passport, Mrs. Stanford?"

The clerk stepped away to consult a manager. "I'm afraid, Mrs. Stanford, that we are overbooked on your reservation. But we can offer an upgrade to First Class, if that is agreeable."

"How much would that be?"

"No charge. It will be with compliments of Lufthansa. Mr. Armbruster travels with us often and requested the upgrade. And we always give preference to families of our own veterans when we have extra seats."

Rosa sighed, first with confusion, then delight.

She had barely sipped her coffee at the announcement of First Class boarding. She felt a burning blush on her cheeks, guilty that someone might have overheard that she had special treatment.

She was directed onto the 140 seat Boeing 707 jetliner, and a steward ushered her to a second row window seat. With her coat taken and hung in the closet, a silver tray of orange juice and coffee was offered at her seat even before the economy cabin had boarded.

"Orange juice, please."

Yes—this is the life. And a vacant seat beside me too.

In Rosa's world, she was always the server and never the served, and this felt awkward at the outset. Yet she enjoyed the luxury of the reclining leather armchair and pull-up foot rest.

Within seconds the attendant was back with a selection of magazines for the overnight flight, and she placed a *Life* and *Redbook* on the empty seat.

Business travelers were boarding in First Class as well, many in pairs or singles, and all men, with some appearing confused at her presence in the front cabin. Many had pipes or cigars to Rosa's disgust, and she decided she could overlook the inconvenience.

When every confirmed reservation was on board, a trickling of standby passengers filed in with carry-ons, many with wrapped Christmas packages for the overhead bin.

A military lieutenant in uniform took the aisle seat beside Rosa. "Good day, Ma'am." He tipped his hat and handed it to the steward.

"Good morning," she replied with a shy smile.

"Are you going to Frankfurt on business or pleasure?"

"A matter of family business, and you?"

"I'm returning to my base in Frankfurt. I've been on leave to attend to a family emergency."

The Captain's announcement of their imminent departure interrupted them, and two stewardesses demonstrated the padded flotation board under the seat and the oxygen bag drop.

Rosa turned away to watch out the window as the great beast rambled and sped down the runway, and lifted, then soared into the air over Queens.

The sudden buoyancy made her lightheaded, and she sat back into the soft leather and became engrossed in a *Life* magazine war story. She glanced to the side over her reading glasses, hoping the lieutenant was now finished with his small chat.

From the seat pocket, Rosa opened a map of Germany with markings of the rail lines. Mr. Armbruster assured her he would be waiting in Frankfurt to assist her to Heidelberg. He'd be wearing a brown felt fedora and a navy wool coat with a nametag. She was both grateful and amused by his concessions.

I wonder what kind of man he is. His voice is strong with authority as he was persuasive and reassuring. I envision a short, stodgy man with a broad face . . . maybe a thick mustache, striking in demeanor, but not what any women would consider to be handsome. If Abel Brand chose him as the family attorney, he must be a good man.

"Excuse me, Ma'am. Your dinner menu is in the pocket. I'll be along shortly for your meal request, but first we'd like to offer a glass of Riesling or Bordeaux."

"Thanks, I'll look at it. Ice water would be fine."

The lieutenant poked her arm gently. "The wine is free and I recommend the Riesling. It's sweet, but refreshing. Many Germans drink wine with every meal."

"I don't know why, but I presumed it would be beer. Thanks for the suggestion, but it's too early for me for wine."

"It's a long flight, and they'll be by often."

Rosa returned to the *Life* article of the tunnel escape from East Berlin led by Erwin Becker, a chauffeur for East German Parliament. Over the page was the February exchange of an American CIA spy, Francis Gary Powers, in return for Rudolph Abel, convicted of spying in the U.S.

In interviews, Powers talked about solitary confinement and his occasions in the population of other airmen captured by the Soviets at Dallgow-Döberitze, a POW camp at Brandenburg in East Germany. He referenced several prisoners including the name Moretti, a man who was tortured, but remained faithful to his country by withholding information.

Rosa stewed over it.

Something about that name . . . it's significant in my memory.

She looked up as the stewardess arrived, and opted for a garden salad and chicken pot pie.

"Perhaps a cup of tea too if it's not too much trouble."

"Certainly, Mrs. Stanford."

The lieutenant poked her again. "The steak is much tastier. I've flown this route a number of times."

"Thanks for your suggestion," she answered with reduced enthusiasm. "I'll stick with the chicken."

"Suit yourself," the lieutenant chided. Rosa felt his glances as she read, and he confirmed it with a polite compliment of her chestnut brown hair and blue eyes. She buried her thoughts deeper in the article with barely a nod.

"Mrs. Stanford, you said you were traveling on family business. Will you be staying in Frankfurt?"

Rosa wondered how he knew her name, but recalled the stewardess using it and labeling her coat.

"My attorney has made my travel and accommodation arrangements," Rosa said abruptly, hoping it to be the end.

"My apologies for prying. I'm returning from burying my father in New York and I confess I jabber too much to ease my stresses."

The lieutenant seemed sincere and Rosa eased up. "I'm sorry. I know what it's like to lose a loved one. My husband was an airman in Germany. Do you recall ever meeting Jake Stanford? I wonder if he was in Frankfurt during your duty."

"Stanford . . . sorry it doesn't ring a bell. What type of aircraft did he fly?"

"Something like a 152."

"I've heard of it, but as I recall it didn't have a particularly good flight record."

"No, it didn't."

Rosa wasn't expecting any further information from the lieutenant and turned to look out the window at clouds over the Atlantic, with the lights of New York left miles behind.

With dinner cleared, the cabin lights dimmed and the stewardess brought flat pillows and blankets, and a night mask and ear plugs.

Rosa knew she needed rest, but under her lamp, she thumbed through *Arthur Frommer's Europe on $5 a Day* from the airport gift shop. Heidelberg would be an hour's distance on landing, and she was intrigued by the handbook's photos of the whimsical Christmas market in the center of Altstadt, a term for Old Town. She saw budget hotels as low as $3 a day, and three-course German meals a mere 90 cents, with the more historic hotels looking out toward the ancient castle.

With a pencil, she marked sightseeing highlights on a map of walking tours, and circled the historic bridge.

"Edgar and Will would find it captivating—the magic of a winter wonderland and Christmas village all in one. I already miss them after a few hours." She closed her eyes to envision Mrs. Fitch saying prayers and tucking in the boys, and moments later she drifted to sleep.

In no time, the cabin lights went up again as breakfast trays were delivered. The German terrain was green through light clouds as they neared Frankfurt. Returning from the restroom, Rosa struggled to fit her train case back into the overhead, and relented at the lieutenant's insistence on helping.

"My feet are swollen," she whispered to herself. "Squeezing them back into my shoes is a battle." Her memory flashed back. As a girl, when her parents couldn't afford new shoes, she insisted the one olds were fine and endured the pinching until her mother noticed her blisters.

The lieutenant overheard her and doled out his experience. "I've learned not to take my shoes off. Don't worry, Mrs. Stanford. Walking down the ramp, the swelling will disappear."

She nodded thanks. "Do you go directly to an army base?"

"I'm due to check in right away . . . and you?"

"I'll be met and go directly to Heidelberg."

"Oh, lucky you! It bursts with character at Christmas." He paused. "Perhaps I'll see you on a future flight."

Leaving the immigration and luggage hall, Rosa stepped into the noise and chaos of a room packed with carts, passengers and greeters.

Gaining her bearings, she scanned the room, settling on a man in a navy, woolen coat and brown felt fedora. Not much more than thirty, he was tall, dark and handsome— and their eyes met before she saw her printed name on his placard.

"Mrs. Stanford!"

"Did Mr. Armbruster send you?"

"I am indeed Adam Armbruster, here in the flesh." His smile was warm and she found she was instantly relaxed.

"Thank you so much for your kindness sending me the advance and coming all this way from Heidelberg to meet me."

His eyes twinkled with the knowledge that she was upgraded. "I hope you had a pleasant flight."

"Yes, very pleasant. You have been generous with details, Mr. Armbruster."

"Please, now that we are face to face, call me Adam."

"Thank you, Adam. You know I'm Rosa."

She carried her small case, and he took her valise.

A blast of cold air preceded a flurry of snowflakes, both as she would have imagined.

"I have a hired car waiting to take us to the train station," Adam said, and stepped forward to hold open the passenger door of a black sedan.

The driver seemed anxious, and conversed in German at length with Adam, who then became silent in thought.

"It seems that two trains have collided at the Frankfurt train station and a backlog may take hours to clear. If you agree, the driver is willing to take us to Heidelberg by car."

Seeing the exhaustion on her face, he nodded to the driver. With a slight shudder, Rosa laid her head back to watch the scenery as they left Frankfurt. The relief of ending a long journey was setting in and she allowed her eyes to grow heavy again with slumber.

Half an hour later, the attorney nudged her.

"Mrs. Stanford . . . Rosa, we are approaching Heidelberg and you won't want to miss the spectacular view."

With her eyes still closed, she spoke up with her motherly instincts, "Edgar, is Will alright?"

"I'm sure your boys are fine. You've been napping, that's all."

"I apologize for my rudeness, Mr. Armbruster."

"Adam . . . and no need."

Rolling hills and tall forests surrounded Heidelberg, nestled between Odenwald and the Upper Rhine Graben. On the foggy window, Rosa's finger traced a wet circle, and on the outside, streams of melting snow trickled on the glass.

As they passed the river dividing the town in two, the afternoon sun was projecting onto the buildings, with the sky turning orange and the famous castle enamored with lights.

"It's the Neckar . . . the river, I mean," Adam said, watching her eyes. "It's built as a canal through the center. And you must ride the funicular cable car from upper to lower town; ours was the first, but many other cities have them now.

"I wish my boys were here. The town is magical already."

"Our universities are in demand and there's always a waitlist for apartments and rooms to let. Your hotel has a view of the castle. It's central to walk anywhere without transit, so you can go often to the bridge and to the gastronomic area and shops."

"Thank you, Adam. That is so thoughtful."

Saying his name out loud seemed odd to her.

I'm a widow with two children.

Adam interrupted her brief trance. "If you decide to take any day trips on the Hauptbahnhof, it is only a few blocks from Old Town and the trains are frequent. Many people ski in the mountains on weekends. What about you? Do you ski?"

"Who me?" She laughed at the visual.

"Afraid not. I was born and raised in the metropolis of New York. We don't have the luxury of countryside, unless you count the parks."

The sedan pulled up to a pink building with a grand and splendid façade.

"This is it, the Hotel Hollander Hof. I picked it for its romantic old-world charm, but with modern conveniences."

Adam carried Rosa's valise to check-in, and her key was already ready in an envelope.

"All set, you're on the third floor. The elevator only takes one or two at a time, so you might prefer the stairs in a hurry. There's plenty of time to relax before I return at seven."

He blushed. "I hope you don't object that I was too presumptuous, as I've booked a dinner reservation."

"It sounds perfect to me, Adam."

Through the elevator doors, she watched him in the lobby.

What a handsome gentleman. Not the stodgy man I imagined.

She was certain he took a look back.

5

Matters of Abel Brand's Estate, Heidelberg

*A*t the sight of the superior room, Rosa grinned with pleasure that Adam had made this special effort for her. She placed her bag in the spacious sitting area by the writing desk. The ambiance was beyond what she had expected, with spotless white walls, and rosewood accents on the doors and framing.

Sprawling onto the double bed, her shoes fell ungracefully to the floor and she let her body sink into the down comforter. A blissful wave enveloped her, and she raised her head slightly toward the window.

Yes, darkness is descending. I can't believe it was yesterday that I left New York. I imagine Mrs. Fitch has made a generous dinner for the boys and they'll be watching Christmas cartoons. I've never left them for more than an evening before.

Choosing a silk, navy frock with white petunias woven into the fabric, she preened at the mirrored wardrobe.

Shoulder pads with sleeves cuffed at the elbow made her look thinner, but she knew the truth. Brushing until she had smooth curls, she touched a tweak of rouge to her cheeks, then a careful line of cranberry red lipstick.

She wondered if a hat would be right for dinner tonight; she brought two, one for travel and the other for a special occasion should it arise. It was a peculiar sensation that she wrestled with, in the anticipation of dining with another man, without Jake there.

"Forgive me, Jake. I do this all for you and your family."

She knew it was a lie—that she was in desperate financial need. Raising two young boys and without a military pension, it had been a battle to pay the bills. She whispered again that it was for her boys.

With stomach butterflies, she took the staircase to the lobby. It was 6:45 p.m. and she'd be prompt and exact as her way. She spotted Adam as she arrived, and their eyes met in an instant of awkwardness and fluster. He recovered first.

"You look lovely, Rosa."

She gripped his extended arm.

"I didn't bring the car as it's only a few blocks. The moon is barely visible and we can endure a wisp of snowflakes."

Rosa glanced at the parcel under his arm.

"Oh yes, Rosa. Before we go . . . this is for you for this snowy night. In Heidelberg, women wear fashionable scarves swirled over their heads. I picked a practical and colorful one that might go with anything in your wardrobe." Instantly he regretted saying 'practical'.

She tilted her head to hide her bashful smirk, and unfolded the brown wrapping. It was a finely woven, wool scarf with Christmas motif in red, green, and blue, as big as a shawl.

"It's splendid, Adam. Really."

At a lobby mirror, she let the scarf fall over her curls and swept it under her chin, with the fringe flowing behind.

"Did I do it correctly?"

Adam beamed without a reply.

The night air was invigorating on the stroll to Old Bridge Square.

They stopped in front of a yellow painted stucco building with dark rose trim and inviting windows, the Wirtshaus Zum Nepomuk restaurant, in an 18th century townhouse on Platz vor der Alten Brücke. It had a view of the Neckar River and the castle, and she recalled it from Mr. Frommer's book.

"I was hoping you'd like dining here tonight, Rosa. Aside from the best German fare, they're known for Italian and French, and recently added a Michelin star to their credit."

Rosa nodded her pleasure and silent curiosity of Michelin. All she knew was that this was all incredible. Inside, her eyes fell across the room, at the natural wood, and the crisp linens and sparkling crystal. At a checkerboard-clothed table, a single rose waited at her plate beside an amber lantern. She raised her eyes toward other tables, realizing each had a flower of some sort.

Adam held her chair as Jake used to do.

"Thank you, Adam. You have been extremely kind to me."

"Well, this is an important business meeting. I wanted you to have a favorable opinion of Heidelberg as the home of your husband's ancestors."

Yes, it is only a business meeting.

With water glasses filled, a formal wine steward presented himself with the slightest bow of his head. Adam looked toward Rosa. "Do you enjoy a glass of Riesling?"

Thank goodness for the lieutenant.

"Oh yes, that would be perfect."

She watched Adam approve the taste, and eased back in her chair as the glasses were filled. In a flash, the steward was back with leather-bound menus, one in German, and the other with English translation.

"Rosa, I should tell you that fried carp is our traditional dish, but many tourists look for Viennese schnitzel with spätzle. However, you can ask for anything you desire."

"Thank you, Adam, but I'm more than a bit overwhelmed. Would you please make a selection for me that a girl from Queens might enjoy?"

"Certainly, Rosa. I'd say crisp roasted duck with dumplings and red cabbage for you. Myself . . . I'd like the carp."

"That sounds scrumptious."

After an apple strudel, Adam's face became stern.

"Rosa, tomorrow we will go to the Brand haus and I will explain the details of the estate. Do you mind if we briefly discuss your husband?"

She hoped her face didn't show her pain as she nodded her agreement.

"As required by law, our firm posted in local newspapers for three weeks, requesting any information of the whereabouts of Jacob George Stanford, an American pilot missing in action. We got the normal curious fortune hunters that were easy to weed out. But one peaked my interest."

"What was it?" she asked.

"It was from an Italian pilot. He said he was on a flight with your Jake when the plane went down."

Rosa gasped and her eyes watered.

"What was his name?"

In a flash, the *Life* magazine article came back, and she knew it would be Moretti.

"Vincenzo Moretti."

She knew the words were coming, but it was still like a ton of bricks, and she began to tremble.

Adam reached across the table and laid his hand on hers. "It's alright, Rosa, we'll get this sorted out. I know you need to know what happened to your husband. Trust me to guide you through."

Rosa looked up into his compassionate eyes and was struck by how green they were.

Just like Jake's.

"How much information did Moretti supply? Did Jake eject from the plane? Was he captured? Did they turn over his body? This is all too much, Adam."

"Can we walk? It always clears the thoughts."

Out in the square, she was oblivious to the spectacular sights of the night lights on the castle. They mixed with the crowds meandering on the bridge, and passed swooning couples tying keys of remembrance and love onto the handrail.

She leaned against Adam's arm, grasping a bit of security, and her eyes glistened at the brilliant reflections of Christmas lights and kiosks.

Adam didn't initiate the conversation while they walked, but at a park with an illuminated carousel, he insisted they sit on a bench.

"Rosa, you should know that he did escape from the plane crash."

"I don't believe that."

"Here's what we found. Jacob was wounded when he was first taken prisoner by the Soviets. Later, he was separated from Moretti in an East German concentration camp. Although the air force hasn't provided concrete proof, the co-pilot says he heard that Jacob tried to escape recently. I'm sorry, Rosa. He was killed. Moretti can give us the date and location."

Her eyes watered but she stayed composed. "Is that really true. Are you continuing to investigate?"

She knew the answer and gripped his arm tighter. "Thank you, dear Adam."

He waited with her for the tiny elevator to open at the lobby level, as they both knew her legs were too wobbly for the staircase.

"Adam, it must have been difficult for you to tell me this. I'll be fine for our meeting tomorrow."

"If you change your mind, call me. Otherwise I'll come for you at about 10 a.m."

Shuddering with exhaustion, Rosa took a deep breath and let the lift take her out of the moment. Adam stayed until the doors closed, wondering if he could have softened the blow.

6

Visit to BrandHaus, Heidelberg

Rosa woke with the load lifted from her shoulders. In her heart, the words rang through that Jake was no longer alive, yet she clung to her memories of a gentle, loving husband and father. She had never before given thought to life without ever seeing Jake again.

On her pillow, she reread the *Life* item over and over, now more interested in the co-pilot Moretti.

With a host of questions for Adam, she dressed quickly. The smell of coffee wafted up the stairway, and flavored aromas welcomed and drew her to the breakfast room.

"Good morning, Mrs. Stanford. We're glad you will join us, and of course breakfast is included with your room."

Half the tables were occupied, but she settled at a quiet one. The sight of the elaborate buffet triggered her appetite and she poured herself a coffee and picked a croissant with apricot spread. The attendant met her at the table and pulled her chair.

"Mrs. Stanford, you must have the omelette. Our cook will make it for you right away."

"Yes, please. Spinach, tomato and feta cheese?"

"It will be only a few minutes."

Despite a ravenous appetite, Rosa picked through the fruit and cheese like a bird, with nerves having set in about what the day might bring. She was accustomed to order in her life, and wanted to establish bench posts to accept her future. She was ready now to see Adam and deal with the business aspect of her journey. There would be time for grief later.

At 9:55, she was in the lobby when he arrived.

"Are we walking today?" she asked.

"Yes indeed. We only need to go four blocks to the clock shop, and we'll start there."

"Perfect, I need to buy a cuckoo clock for my neighbor for looking after my boys."

Rosa took his arm and they started in the direction of the castle.

"Sometime you must show me pictures of Edgar and Will."

"Of course. Thanks for asking that."

Near the Old Town square, they slowed past the limestone buildings, packed with colorful shops. Many were wedged into narrow spaces, with windows bordered by hand-painted Christmas decorations and baubles. Stopping outside the pastry shop, they marveled over delicate macarons and strudel, then moved on to the frosted window of a toy maker's shop, with Pinocchio puppets and wooden bears outside, refreshing the imagination of her own childhood.

The high glass storefront of the clockmaker presented a menagerie of regulator wall clocks, pendulum cuckoos and spinning brass anniversary pieces. Inside, they were met by an imposing hand-carved grandfather clock from another era.

For Rosa, it was a ticking world of whimsy, and she was momentarily spell-bound by the new feeling of belonging to such ancestral craftsmanship.

Adam stood back, giving her time to absorb the revelation.

"Oh, Adam, it is another world."

"Indeed it is. Your husband's family has owned this for several generations. However, as Abel Brand aged, he made an agreement with a loyal clockmaker, Ludwig Bachmann, to sell one half. He is the clockmaker that wishes to buy out the estate's share. I'm sure, if you decide to agree, he will provide you with your cuckoo clock."

"Yes, of course. This shop should be run by a clockmaker and most certainly the one of Abel's choosing. I'll be ready to see the agreement you suggest."

"In its time, Rosa. We'll look at the rest of the building first before you make any decisions. Three floors of apartments are above this shop, with three on each floor— two each front facing and one at the back with a terrace. They all have tenant lease agreements with Herr Brand, except for his own residence that is unoccupied on the second floor. I have a waitlist for potential renters, as well as an offer from an hotelier to gut and renovate the entire building."

"Do you have a key with you for the Brand residence?"

With a pocket pat, Adam grinned. "Shall we take the stairs?"

"You don't suggest there's an elevator in this old building?"

"No, I'm only poking a bit of fun." They both laughed at their ease together.

The staircase and halls were dark without natural daylight, but dim wall sconces hung at each landing and a chandelier dangled from the tall ceiling. The hardwood steps were shiny and worn from past generations over its hundred years. In front of apartment 2A was a boot-brushing mat imprinted 'Herzlich Willkommen'.

"What does that say, Adam?"

"It's a welcome mat."

She rolled her eyes with a petite and feminine snort. "Of course. And I must buy a translation book."

Adam slipped a folder out from an inside pocket. "That's solved—I bought one for you. But everyone in Heidelberg speaks English, so you might not even open it."

Unlocking the door, Rosa was transported to a bygone era of antiques and warmth. With the curtains closed, the air was musty, but she immediately felt at home. In the parlor, she watched as Adam pulled the drapes back for daylight and turned on the lamps.

Instinct told her the worn armchair would be where Abel sat to look out at the lights of the Christmas market. Sinking deep, she reached for a padded leather album on the side table with a hand-painted inscription, 'Brand Family'. Adam was rooting in the kitchen for a kettle and a tea canister, and she called out as he lit the gas burner.

"It's too lovely, Adam. There's nothing more to say than that." She thumbed through pages of aged Kodak photos of family gatherings, but stopped, thunderstruck by one of Eve Brand holding her infant son that sent shivers up her spine. Lifting it from its corner tucks, she examined it by the lamp.

It's like you're right here with me, Jake.

Turning the page, a folded paper fluttered to the floor, and her eyes grew wide with excitement, then apprehension.

"It's for me!"

Scrawled by an arthritic hand was her name, Rosa Stanford.

Adam stayed by the kettle, knowing that it was only a matter of time before she found the letter, and that the words would be painful. As she unfolded the letter, she recognized the writing as Jake's.

Dearest Rosa,

I had a nostalgic visit with Granddad at his home in Heidelberg, and told him much about you, my beautiful Rosa, and our two boys. We promised each other that we would meet again soon.

Old Abel is weakening and I saw he had difficulty now climbing the stairs. I fear his days are numbered, and being with him I realize that mine are too.

Every day we go up, Russian MiGs swarm our plane, firing on us. I dream at night in the barracks, imagining a Soviet firing squad—in it, I'm running and hiding and wherever I go the Gestapo is there with rifles. The people of East Germany live in fear every day, and escape is almost impossible. I can barely remember peace times.

I write this on the morning of a new mission with the phantom 152. Its maiden flight had engine malfunctions, so although I have confidence, I know there's increased risk. If for any reason the war prevents me from returning home, please embrace the German heritage of our sons, and find love and joy again. You will always be in my heart, and I will watch over you from Heaven.

Love forever, your Jake

P.S. I am giving this letter to Vincenzo. We've now been taken prisoner at Dallgow-Döberitze in Havilland near Brandenburg. With my wounds, my mobility won't let me join Moretti in a plan that I can't write about. I'll tell you later.

The page was badly soiled, with the corner smeared with stains of bloodied fingerprints. Placing the letter on her lips, she kissed his loving words before she allowed the barrage of pain to unexpectedly hurl her body into violent sobbing.

Morelli's escape plan with the Americans. This is a farewell letter!

Adam was relieved with the whistle of the kettle. He allowed her the intimacy of space with her feelings, but admonished himself—perhaps he shouldn't have placed the letter there, and hoped she'd forgive him that he knew beforehand.

When the sobbing eased, Rosa folded it at the same creases, and turned to the window to hide her tear-streaked cheeks. Adam approached quietly with her tea, in a delicate gold-trimmed cup and hand-painted saucer.

She looked into his eyes and saw both compassion and an unexplained sadness.

"I'll be alright. There was a letter in the album from Jake. It came as a shock. What do you know of the man named Moretti?"

Adam dreaded the question, yet she waited for his answer.

"Rosa . . . Abel Brand was a kind, gentle man. When he received the diagnosis that his time was short, he confided in me and pleaded that I get Jake, and you of course, to come to Heidelberg after his passing. He longed for his family, and was proud of his roots and wanted assurances that he'd be remembered by the next generation."

He hesitated as she showed patience with him.

"But that's not what you are asking of me… you want to know about Moretti. To be frank, he replied to my newspaper posting and came to Heidelberg to meet with me. He's the one that brought the letter and I placed it in a safe place. As I told you earlier, I didn't intend to cause you undue anguish."

"Adam, I only met you yesterday but I quickly learned that you too are a kind and honorable man. I can understand Abel Brand placing his trust in you, and I have now done the same. It must be a burden for you and I am sorry for that, but I must have answers that will allow me to go forward in life. Do I seek a ghost or do I grieve the past and begin again for the sake of my boys?"

Adam swallowed hard on his guilt. She had taken everything he said at face value and not second-guessed him even once. The telegram to her had been easy and she had not even asked the name of the law firm.

"Until the remains of Captain Stanford are returned to you, the question will haunt you. Your husband would not want it to antgonize and defeat you."

"How would you know what my husband would want?" As the words spurted, she regretted that the flash of anger escaped.

Adam wanted to tell the truth but instead turned away.

"Please forgive me, Adam. I didn't mean to sound harsh. I have anger inside that I don't know what to do with."

"Perhaps this is enough of the Brand estate for today. There's a skating rink close to Old Town on the Karlsplatz. Do you skate?"

Rosa burst into laughter. "It's been a few years, when I was a girl. In all the years Jake and I were married, we never went skating. But it would be amusing at least, and exercise can relieve tension. Adam, I fear that I am taking up all your time. You must have other clients."

"Don't give it a thought. I am attached to a family firm. I am a widower without children so my evenings are generally lonely. My brothers will pick up the slack, and we agreed beforehand that settling the Brand estate for Abel would be my priority while you are here. Suppose we walk back to your hotel and you can change for skating. We can rent skates and have a few spins."

The night air was invigorating. At an island at the center of the ice, an enormous Christmas tree was bedecked with brilliant sparkling lights and shimmering gold balls.

A classical jig piped out to lure skaters to the rink, with the bravest attempting a waltz. Uneasy at first, Rosa convinced her weak ankles to venture a first step. She reached for Adam and let her weight fall against his arm. It was the first time she didn't feel guilty for depending on him.

"Adam, I think the Brand house should be my home while I am here. Is that alright?"

His hand gripped hers tighter so she couldn't fall. "I was hoping you'd say that. We'll check you out of the Hollander in the morning and get you settled in there. If you're up to it tomorrow, we can go over the documents and make a few decisions."

7

Confessions of Vince Moretti, Heidelberg

That night, Rosa tossed and turned with nightmares of Jake running with gunfire rattling behind him. It was a vision of him in slow motion towards her across a bridge, with his hand stretched out trying to grasp hers. As hard as she tried she couldn't reach him, and the frustration forced her to tears until she sat upright in bed. Each time she returned to sleep, Jake was there again, reaching for her.

I love you, dear Jake. I don't want to spend my years chasing a ghost. I need a sign.

Even before breakfast, she was packed and eager to move to the apartment over the clock store. Waiting with a coffee in a lobby chair, she scanned a brochure of Christmas events, Advent services and candlelight traditions in Old Town. It hadn't occurred to her that many churches would be

Lutheran-Protestant, as her own family was Roman Catholic, with generations at St. Mary's.

From the door, Adam saw she was engrossed. At her chair, he spoke her name softly, not to startle her.

"I'm sorry, Adam. I'm daydreaming, I confess."

"Well, you look packed and ready." In a flash, he was reminded of his feelings from the evening, and how quickly she was capturing his attention.

"Yes, shall we walk?"

"If you feel up to it." Dark lines had circled under her eyes and he presumed she had a difficult night.

"It's a new day and I'm ready to face the world."

Holding her valise, he offered his other elbow. "I arranged for my mother's cleaning service to ready the apartment so the place will be what you Americans say 'spic and span'."

Rosa laughed at his attempt to relate in American anecdotes. "Spic and span . . . I like that."

Without a deadline, they sauntered under the morning flurries, at last seeing the clock shop ahead.

"How did Abel Brand die? Was he in the hospital suffering for long?"

"We'll discuss that over a pot of tea if you like at the Brand house, and we can review the details and documents."

It was the first indication to Rosa that Adam was skirting her questions. His face tightened and he didn't offer the same understanding eyes to appease her concerns.

Is it my imagination, or is he not even looking at me?

They stopped at a stuffed postal rack in the hall leading up to the apartments. Adam sorted through and kept a handful of Brand mail, returning the rest for other tenants.

He hadn't spoken in the minutes since Rosa had prodded for information.

At the landing, he dug her apartment skeleton key from his pocket and kept a second one. As she unpacked, Adam set the kettle and spread a raft of documents on the kitchen table. In front of her chair, he placed a pot covered by an embroidered cozy, with two mugs, a sugar bowl and creamer.

"My mother left enough food to get you started. She wants everything to be ideal and natural for you."

"Tell her she succeeded please, and thank her. Will I have the privilege of meeting her?"

Adam put his hand on his chin and stepped back, then answered quickly. "Perhaps." She let his hesitation pass, as he continued to lay out his files in symmetrical order, to be his order of discussion.

His temple pulsed as he thought, and his jaw tightened; a lock of dark hair had fallen loose over his forehead.

There's something bothering him. Perhaps something I said.

After a large gulp of tea, Adam looked Rosa straight in the eye. "I have something to tell you, Rosa . . ." He stirred his tea unnecessarily, and she waited and watched his green eyes, the ones that reminded her of Jake.

"I am the attorney that Abel Brand asked to attend to estate matters. The law firm is Armbruster & Sons after my father and grandfather. I did receive a letter from Vince Moretti. All the legal responsibilities that I mentioned yesterday are true. But . . ." He stopped again.

"What is it, Adam? You're scaring me."

"No, Rosa, I don't mean to do that at all. When your husband came to meet with his grandfather, I was here. He talked for a long time about how wonderful you were. I confess I felt envy to see a man so much in love with the woman of his dreams. He talked about you incessantly and I imagined what you would be like and it is exactly as he said. Even down to the way your little finger extends when you hold your tea cup. I remember details, like Jake did."

"Why would you withhold that information from me? It makes no difference."

"But it does, Rosa. Abel Brand was my grandfather too." Compassionate eyes burrowed into her soul and she felt a new sensation she wasn't prepared for.

Rosa was on her feet with her mouth open but no words would come.

"Please Rosa, sit down. There's more, if you let me explain."

"Are you brothers?"

"Not brothers . . . no, no. Jake is my cousin. Abel's wife, Angelina, and her daughter Eve died in a Nazi concentration camp. My mother Florentine was Eve's only sister, and she married my father, Bogdan Armbruster. I always lived in Heidelberg, and Jake and I spent our childhood years adoring Granddad. We shared many stories. Someday, perhaps, I can reveal more to you, if you like."

"Did you have intentions of bringing me all the way from New York on false pretenses? Tell me everything."

"Abel Brand did die four weeks ago. He mourned the loss of his family and valued those that remained. Abel himself went to a rendezvous near Brandenburg Gate. Word had been smuggled to him from Jacob that he planned to escape with others through an underground tunnel under the wall.

"You understand, Rosa, that I am telling you that Jake was alive a month ago."

Rosa felt faint and sat back, nodding slowly. "Did Abel die there then?"

"Abel waited in the bushes on the Western side. But it went badly . . . the Gestapo gunned Abel down in the escape car, and in the aftermath there were others. I'm afraid Jake didn't make it. I'm sorry."

She bolted from her chair to the window with her arms crossed. Her tears were streaming but she stood without moving. Finally and still with her back to Adam, she muttered, "So that's why I see Jake in your eyes."

Adam pretended he didn't hear.

"Abel told me of the plan and I didn't take it seriously. I now sleep with guilt every night for my grandfather and my cousin. He asked me to find you if anything happened to him. It was important as his last wish to me. As a matter of honor and my conscience, I am trying to do that.

"Rosa, your boys are the only bloodline of the next generation. My brother and I haven't been blessed to have children of our own."

Rosa heard the agony in Adam's voice and wanted to comfort him, but she couldn't move. By nature, she was a passionate and sensitive woman.

Adam was still at the table and she heard his chair slide back. "Perhaps, Rosa, it will be best if I leave for now. We can resume the business aspect later, when you are ready."

She still couldn't face him as her voice gained strength. "Adam, don't go. I don't want to go through this alone. It's like I've lost Jake all over again."

She thought she heard his steps retreat into the parlor, but the warmth of his body told her he was standing behind her.

"Rosa, I can't fix this and I don't know what to do to help."

"At this moment, you're family," she said, "and family sticks together. When I saw you at the airport, you reminded me of Jake, but I shirked the feeling. It's too much at once."

"It might help to rest here and feel the presence in this house to connect you. When you're ready, you should call me at this number."

Rosa pivoted at the click of the door and picked up his card. From the window she saw him walk across the cobblestone courtyard in the direction opposite of the castle, and a veil of loneliness returned, more than she'd felt for a long time.

So I am a widow all over again. It has been a difficult passage in life.

Returning to the photo album, she thought if she could find a glimpse of Jake as a child, she'd feel closer. Turning the pages, her finger and curiosity ran through many spaces with empty corners where photos had been removed.

The album pictures were black and white, and those with Christmas trees and family gatherings drew her greatest interest. She guessed they were dated soon after the start of the Second World War when children could still smile.

The Christmas setting in the photos is in this very residence.

By the window was a tinseled Christmas tree with a row of young children perched in front with the broadest smiles. In the chair where Rosa now sat was Granddad Abel, with Angelina perched on his arm rest. On the glossy white space under the photo were words in faded ink: 'Adam, Jacob, Hans and Carolina – Christmas 1942'.

Her gaze was transfixed, when an idea struck her. Adam said the only thing remaining from the original house was the grandfather clock, a hundred year old tall case with tubular chimes. She stood to admire its hand-carving in Black Forest mahogany with a boxwood inlay. The front panel was locked.

I'll search later for the key, it must be somewhere here. As I remember, Jake always hid Christmas presents in places I would never look, like the garret or basement rafters. Once it was a loose chimney brick and another time he flipped off the fireplace mantle and mortared it back into place."

Instinctively, she walked to the fireplace letting her fingers travel every brick looking for crumbling or ease of movement. Over the hearth, she was rewarded by a protrusion of an off-coloured brick. With kitchen tongs, she pulled it to get a grip, then heard the crunch of paper and peered in behind.

The page was brittle, and the letter in childish writing and in German that she couldn't read. She calculated that it must have been from about the same time as the photos with the Christmas tree, 1942.

Poor sweet Jake. This would have been his last Christmas in Heidelberg. Perhaps I can make one more.

With the apartment on the second floor, there was no usable attic or basement for storage. Finding no decorations, Rosa's determination was bolstered to bring Christmas and life back to this house. She wrapped Adam's scarf over her head and scurried out into the flurries, returning with colored bags bursting with parcels, and her arms heavy with pine boughs.

With joy like a child, she laid out the Advent calendar and placed miniature wrapped chocolates in each enveloped slot. She then hastened to polish the window, and hung the

Advent candles to glow out onto the street to the shoppers below.

On tiptoes on a chair, she hung boughs of garland over the entrance and window frames, and attached golden balls and angels. Beside Abel's chair, she set a miniature porcelain Christmas tree with lights, and on the table she laid out cakes, cookies and Christmas stollen and covered them with saran.

There you go, Jake. This is your last Christmas and I'm here with you.

Adam didn't call all that afternoon, yet she waited by the phone hoping to hear his voice. Turning on the old Marconi, she listened to Bing Crosby's *I'll be Home for Christmas*, a tune from near the end of the war. It was a symbol of hope for returning soldiers, telling those at home to get ready with snow and mistletoe. She hummed it over and over.

Dusk was approaching and she began to worry, with a longing to see Adam.

8

Family Matters, Heidelberg

Through the bedroom curtains, the sunrise filtered over Rosa's eyelids and she sat up to adjust to her surroundings. A cup of tea and a marzipan stollen would have to suffice, with so much on her agenda. With Adam's card, she set out to find his office.

Not more than six blocks away, she stopped in front of a sandstone building, three storeys tall with a metal sign waving in the breeze over the door. A brass plate said it was erected in 1895, and Rosa wondered how long the Armbrusters had been here. Surveying the building, she saw a light in the upper corner office and words in embossed gold distinction on the window, broadcasting Armbruster & Sons, Rechtsanwälte. A man's silhouette moved into her view.

The law office. Is that Adam?

Her heart skipped a beat as she bounded to the second floor. A women in the outer office motioned to come in.

Through a glass partition on a half wall was Adam, hunched over files. His shirt sleeves were rolled part way up his forearm and his tie loosened. With a lock of curls over his forehead, she admired how handsome he was. Appearing frustrated, he leaned back in his chair, crumpled a paper from his desk and tossed it toward a corner bin.

Rosa tapped at his door and Adam looked up with a peculiar expression. "Am I interrupting?" she asked.

"Oh no, you could never be an interruption. I'm glad you're here and I'm so sorry for upsetting you."

"It had to be done and I thought you took a brave plunge. Truce!"

Rosa offered her hand as if to seal a business transaction, and he reached back to hold it, returning a warm smile.

"I'd like to sign whatever documents you have for me. I promised my boys I'd be back in New York in time for Christmas."

Adam's nod hid his dejection that she might leave so soon. "Yes, Edgar and Will. How old are they now?"

"I'll show you," she said with a finger in the air. From her pocket book she flipped to a tiny folio of photos. "This is Edgar, he's seven, and here's Will, barely four. With Jake gone for more than three years, only Edgar has vague memories."

Adam studied their facial expressions. "It's marvelous. They are wonderful. I haven't been fortunate enough to have children of my own."

"You will someday, Adam."

She remembered that he was a widower and regretted she hadn't asked or shown interest about his deceased wife.

"I do apologize. I've allowed you into my life, yet you haven't even mentioned your wife. Has she been gone long?"

At the window, he contemplated his words.

"We were only married a few months when Astrid became ill. It was cancer and she went quickly. Thanks for asking, but I really don't want to talk further about that."

Rosa nodded. "I understand." She saw she had opened an old wound, and moved on quickly.

"You must be wondering why I came this morning."

"I'm glad you're here. I know healing takes time, and I hope you found solitude at the Brand house."

"Yes, but I fretted about the new responsibilities I've agreed to undertake. It seemed like Abel was talking to me, and I had a vivid reminder that Christmas is time for families, joyfulness, and charity.

"I listened to carols till they went off the radio, then drifted to sleep. Before I knew it, morning peeked in to wake me up, and today everything is as clear as a fresh snowfall. Since Jake disappeared three years ago, my life has been a struggle every day to provide."

"I'm sorry, Rosa, and I can understand. Abel and I decided in the Christmas spirit to ease that type of burden as much as we could for folks with needs in Heidelberg, the town that supported him during good times and bad.

"Abel suffered greatly during Hitler's reign and the occupation. You see, the parents of Angelina, my grandmother, were Jewish. During the eradication, anyone suspected of Jewish blood carried cards identifying their bloodlines back to their grandparents.

"I carried one too, but thankfully my father has a strong German ancestry that saved me. Papers were presented to find work, buy food or rent a roof overhead. Angelina's papers kept her under constant suspicion. Jake's mother, my Aunt Eve, went to live with her parents when her husband George died, and although he was English, her bloodline was exposed too."

Adam saw a growing distress on her brow and knew to change the mood. "But you didn't come to hear a sad tale of my ancestry."

"It is important that I know and appreciate Jake's lineage though. I took so much for granted. Later, I hope you'll tell me more."

Adam's warm words were what she needed, and she relaxed. "Indeed I feel it *was* Abel that directed your thoughts at the house. Wait a moment and I'll explain the estate papers."

Rosa draped her coat on a wooden tree and pulled a chair to the desk. The office furniture wasn't matched, and she imagined each piece with its own history and vintage. The credenza behind was piled with stacks of files and leather covered books.

The papers already on the desk were spread in three piles, by category. "You ready?" he sighed.

She pulled herself closer to rest her elbows. For an instant, the aftershave was familiar and she closed her eyes enjoying the sensation of intimacy.

"First there is the clock shop. Ludwig Bachmann was an acquaintance of the Brands for years, and before him was his father, a master craftsman. When the Nazis stole inventory to give to their captains and lieutenants, the Bachmann family escaped, but reclaimed the clock shop after the war.

"Ludwig has now made a generous offer, and Abel has stated his desire to have the Bachmann family continue the tradition of his craft in the shop. He continues the mastery of a dying craft and receives orders from customers and collectors around the world."

"Yes, I'll accept your recommendation, Adam. Would it be too aggressive to ask that he provide me with one cuckoo clock to take back to the United States?"

"I'm certain he would be honored."

"One more thing about clocks. As the grandfather clock at Abel's apartment is original to his family from before the war, I'd like it to remain in the apartment while I'm here, but after that perhaps your family would like to take it. After all, your mother is Abel's daughter. Why didn't she become the heir?"

"When Jake was here, he mentioned the challenges your family faced in New York. Abel and my mother wanted the wisest solution for the estate and agreed it would be best served by helping her nephew and his family. The law firm is well-established and the family home has no mortgage. Our needs are few. We are a charitable family and feel responsibility to see that our own are taken care of."

"Then it's clear you get your responsible, strong character from your mother. But whatever you think of me, Adam, don't consider me a charity case."

His warm eyes gave her assurance and her breathing eased to a smile.

"My mother will dearly treasure the grandfather clock," he said. "She insisted that I bring you to family dinner on Saturday night before church. She's anxious to meet you. After all, you are her sister's daughter-in-law and she thinks of you as a niece."

"It sounds perfect, meeting your family . . . I guess they're a bit mine now too."

"Christmas is so important to us. For four weeks up to it, special events are held Saturdays and Sundays at churches in Heidelberg. Ours is Lutheran—the Providence Church.

"Next, we have the matter of the apartments."

"Could you fill me in about the flats? Do they sell or rent? Are they furnished? How many leases did Abel hold?"

"Accommodation is hard to come by with demand from university students. It's rare when an apartment comes up for sale or lease. Other than Abel's unit, there are seven others. Also, a terrace house is on the roof that needs repair, but it rents as it is. I mentioned earlier that we've had pressure to sell to a hotelier."

"Well, I see plenty of hotels in Heidelberg, and it remains my feeling that Abel would want the building to remain home to others. The developer is out of the question." Rosa heard the assertion in her voice and wondered who this person speaking was.

"You are indeed selfless . . . Jake said you were."

Her face flushed. "Could you explain the waitlist and the circumstances of the applicants?"

"If you want continued income from the estate, rent is preferable. Otherwise, you can liquidate and be done with it. A safety deposit box and bank account are at the Sparkhasse, and we'll go later in the week."

"Of course you should hold back expenses for funerals and travel arrangements and naturally a retainer for the firm's services," she said.

"Rosa . . . there hasn't been a funeral yet."

She was stunned and her voice warbled when she spoke. "I had no idea."

"We've been waiting for you to come and host a memorial service for both Jacob and Abel, only if you wish to do that."

Rosa was visibly shaken, and Adam paused for them both to gather composure.

"My mother hoped that we could have such a memorial service at the church while you're here. Jake is already buried in a military grave, and I'll take you when you're ready.

"Abel had many friends here and significant kinfolk. Also the church social club ladies would assist Mother, if you have no objection."

"I'm moved by their kindness. Yes, it should be at the Providence church . . . and the estate should host a light luncheon reception afterwards, if we can arrange that too."

"I can assure you, it will honor both men appropriately.

"Back to the apartments, Rosa. Two tenants on the second level have asked to purchase their units. They all lived there more than ten years."

"Am I right that Abel would be generous . . . that he'd offer them to the families at reasonable prices that address their financial situations?"

"Why yes, Rosa. That's it exactly. You see his motivation."

"Then there's no question. We'll do that."

Adam jotted the decisions on a pad.

"Another terrace unit at the back is rented by one of the clockmaker's craftsmen from downstairs, and he expressed an interest to buy too. He also does maintenance to keep the building in repair, and for that he gets a rent adjustment."

"Absolutely, he should stay. Same as the first two as long as it is beneficial to the tenants."

"The third floor unit facing the square has three or four students and has turnover every year. As those tenants are transient, the furniture stays. Across the hall, the other front suite is rented by a professional couple, both teachers, with annual contracts at the University."

"Then ensure the student apartment remains available on an annual lease. But after expenses, the rental payments will return to the University as a humanitarian bursary in honor of Abel Brand. Am I making this too complicated?"

"No indeed, it is a labor of love. We're almost there. All that is left is the third floor terrace suite that will be vacant soon, and the roof house rented by a starving artist."

"Adam, would you select someone in need for the terrace suite from your waitlist, either to rent or sell. And for the artist, I applaud someone who tries to make a living from his own talents. His rent or a rent-to-own situation should continue."

Adam admired her acumen and lowered his pen. "This is incredible generosity, Rosa. Abel would be immensely proud."

"Christmas is for benevolence and this one will be remembered by me for many years to come. I haven't told you much about myself. I work at a downtown Manhattan department store. Every day I go to work by bus, train and subway. Standing out in the cold in front of the store is my dear friend, Mr. Harris, who lost a leg in the war. He's never miserable, but has a cheerful greeting every day, and I make sure the change I can spare goes into his charity kettle, even if it's a few coins. We should be helping those in need, especially those that served our country.

"At Christmas, I am humbled by a story my mother read to me. It's about the Gift of the Magi. Do you know it?"

"Yes, where the poor young couple gave up what means most to them to buy a gift for the other. The sacrifice of her tresses and his watch for a comb and a watch chain. It is about giving, and I can see that you would be like that too."

Blushing, she hadn't intended flattery from the tale, and returned to the moment.

"Assuming it all goes as we agreed, there will be rental income. What do you wish to happen to that?"

"I need only a reasonable amount for living expenses and to set up a college fund for Will and Edgar. Beyond a vacation now and then, anything above could go to charity. I don't know now, maybe an orphanage or veterans hospital. A fee should be turned back to Armbrusters' firm for managing it. Did Abel have much debt to clear?"

"Oh no, he didn't agree with the concept of credit or financial obligations. Nothing has accrued to the estate."

Adam looked into her trusting eyes. "For Heidelberg, you are like Santa Claus coming to town."

"Can we celebrate over lunch?" Rosa said.

"Are you asking me for a date?" he teased.

"Oh no, Adam. It is a conclusion of a business meeting."

He didn't feel like her lawyer anymore.

9

Cuckoo Clocks, Heidelberg

Rosa had missed St. Nicholas Day on December 5th when she was still in New York. Dressed in splendid velvet and silks, trimmed with white rabbit fur, the grand gentleman had walked from house to house where he knew eager young children waited.

Under his arm was the enormous ancient book of *Naughty and Nice* where he'd recorded good and bad deeds of the children of Heidelberg over the past year. Always jovial, St. Nicholas offered praise for good deeds and a reprimand for not being honest and humble.

Reading of it, Rosa's imagination transported her back to childhood memories when she had first visited Santa Claus at Macy's.

Every child should be touched by this magical fantasy.

At lunch she brought it up and Adam reminisced about his 1942 Christmas, and a visit from St. Nicholas.

"It was the year in the photo of Jake and me at Granddad's tree. The war had surrounded us and we lived in fear, yet Christmas was a saving dream. St. Nicholas seemed to be nine feet tall when he came to the Brand house, and he carried such drama and flair we were left speechless. If I close my eyes now, I can still hear his heavy footsteps and a grunt at our door, with his sack over his shoulder.

"We waited in the parlor while he chortled and boomed out, 'Frohe Weihnachten!'. It was Merry Christmas, of course, and our small voices echoed it back. Then Father opened the door and Mother and Aunt Eve offered him tea and a morsel of gingerbread. He drank the tea, but refused the gingerbread and broke it into pieces, offering it back to the children who hadn't seen such a delicacy for years.

"At my turn on his knee, he praised me for bringing coal in every morning to stoke the pot belly without being asked, but then came the reprimand. My brother had been relentless one day, flaunting that he was Granddad's favorite. Feeling angry, I swung at him, leaving a bruise on his cheek. I was promptly punished by my father and was completely taken aback that the story had reached St. Nicholas."

"Sounds like he deserved it," Rosa laughed to ease the negativity of the memory.

"Oh no, of course not, but I regret that every day and have never raised my hand to anyone since. Even in the military it was difficult taking up arms in battle."

"There must be something more pleasant about that visit."

"Ah, yes indeed. The mystic of St. Nicholas was not complete without opening a special treat, always a miniature marzipan. It was perfectly created, shaped as a Christmas bell; even now a delight to recall. That night, I left my polished boots outside the door expecting another treat from St. Nick, but in the morning, the treat was a sugar cookie that was much like those in Mother's pantry. The logic was confusing but not devastating, as the mystery and magic remained with me. But I was puzzled even years later about the tall gentleman, as there were no nine-foot Germans in Heidelberg."

"There comes a time like that in every child's life," Rosa said, "but the magic continues through life. Mine definitely."

"When we finish this strudel, I'll take you to the Christmas market to pick out a wreath."

"I had a head start, Adam, as I have already been out shopping and bought the Advent calendar. Abel's room seemed to need it, and the entry does need a wreath."

"Lucy Day is coming on the 13th, the feast of Saint Lucia, the Festival of Lights, about light and growth. A brass band plays carols from the Zum Ritter Hotel balcony, starting up street dancing. "

At the Providence Church, Bach music will remind us of our faith—many times during the war it was the beauty of music or the words of a sermon that kept us going. When we have nothing of physical value, the senses we rely on will get us through. Hunger became satisfied by faith. Lucy Day ignites everyone's hearts with the season's spirit."

"This week, it's like I've been transported to the North Pole and given a new perspective. At Abel's, I hear jingling and singing in my dreams."

"Rosa, it's the most enchanting time to visit Germany, and I can't express my pleasure that you're here."

With his gentle words, she felt at home.

"Adam, I was rooting through things at Abel's and discovered a loose fireplace brick. Stuffed behind was a child's letter in German—would you come by and translate?"

"Of course, but it's time that I teach you a few words too."

Herr Bachmann was outside, sweeping a snow skiff from the steps of the clock store, as if he were watching and waiting for them.

"Good day, Herr Bachmann. It's my honor to introduce Rosa Stanford who has come to help us settle Abel's estate. I meant to call from my office, but I don't have my documents in order yet . . ."

Old Mr. Bachmann interrupted. "Willkommen, Rosa. I did notice a beautiful woman coming and going the last day or two."

Hunched over, the clockmaker neared her slowly to offer his welcome. Slightly stooped from arthritis, Bachmann was a ripe seventy years, but had the spirit of a young man. As he reached for Rosa's hand, she felt a tingle, like a feather tickling her heart.

"It is my pleasure to meet you, Herr Bachmann, as Adam has told me about you and your family. I do hope we'll come to a suitable agreement for you to keep the store. We believe that is what Abel would want. I understand your father and grandfather were master craftsmen as well . . . do you have a son to carry your trade into the next generation?"

Wrinkles on his brow tightened. "I had two sons, both victims of battle; however I then adopted a young man, Franz, who had lost his entire family, and he is proud and keen to carry on the family gift."

"That has to be rewarding," Rosa said.

"May we come in and take a look at your cuckoo clocks, Herr Bachmann?" Adam asked.

"Of course, of course."

The clockmaker stepped aside and held the door. A clock striking three brought a chorus of bells and chimes throughout the store as they entered. Rosa's eyes were wide as she surveyed it, as a whimsical workshop of Santa's elves. Not far inside, she was captivated by a cuckoo's woodsman chopping with his axe, and his wife moving through the red doors with a basket. Two miniature children at the side came forward mechanically to accept it and skip off into the Black Forest.

"I know this one. For certain, it is Hansel and Gretel."

Her eyes on the cuckoo were like a child's on Christmas morning. Adam put his arm around her shoulder to steer her further into the store.

"You can't settle for the first one you see," he teased.

Bachmann beckoned them to a back wall with shelves of mantle clocks and more cuckoos, chirping still.

"Our clocks have skating rinks, and a favorite of mine has sleds filled with children moving over the top and down the carved side. One has a family dining, others with toymakers in Santa's workshop, or elves packing a Christmas sack. Possibly anything you could imagine, my dear. We have the best ones in all of Heidelberg . . . in fact, I like to think in all of Germany."

"You must be proud. It's magnificent and I'm like a child in a candy store."

A bell over the door jangled for Bachmann's attention. "Stay as long as you want, as I have a gentleman to attend to. Patrons first of course," he said with a chuckle.

By three-thirty, Adam whispered they could leave and return for a decision later. Rosa agreed, but stalled again at the alpine cabin in the woods by the door, watching Hansel and Gretel celebrate the half hour.

"Adam, this is the one I want. As a girl, I read every one of Aesop's Fables, but my heart connected to Gretel, the lost girl in the woods."

Adam looked to the back.

"Mr. Bachmann is setting his metronomes right now; we'll come back later."

He called out from the door, "Herr Bachmann, can we meet tomorrow to discuss the estate transaction?"

"I open by nine, but come before we get busy. If we need to meet at your office, I'll arrange for Franz to come in early."

"9 a.m. then. See you here."

Outside, Rosa returned to reality.

It's like I left something back there in the clock shop.

"Thank you, Adam. It was an afternoon I'll remember."

It was time for goodbyes, but Rosa's feet didn't move, and she wondered what on earth she was expecting next.

Adam stepped closer and tucked her scarf into her coat. Their eyes locked and for an instant she thought their souls met. "You take such good care of me. Will I see you again later?"

"Of course. Dinner tonight? My time with you is limited and I won't give up any opportunity."

He so wanted to kiss her but instinct warned him it would be inappropriate. Lingering outside the clock shop, he had second thoughts and returned alone to talk to Herr Bachmann in confidence.

10

Packing up Abel Brand

R osa went about Abel's apartment gathering clothing for the charity shop and emptying drawers. As she bundled shoes in a cardboard box, she started humming. No one would hear her, and she sang a line out loud of *Santa Claus is Coming to Town*.

She stopped suddenly and whispered, "What was that? I'm sure I heard sleigh bells!"

Back in the corner where the wood panels met, she tugged at a fabric tuft.

"It's canvas." Pulling harder yielded more, then the wooden strapping snapped, leaving a gaping hole and more fabric.

Either scared or excited, she decided to wait for Adam's help with the discovery. Instead she set aside keepsakes she thought Florentine could distribute.

Then she came to Angelina's jewelry box. Adam told her that his grandmother had hidden jewels under the floorboards, and that after the Russians left, they were still safe. Inside a heart-shaped locket was a photo of a handsome young couple.

"Yes, that is Angelina, but I shouldn't be doing this. I'll wait for Florentine to come, and if it's not before Saturday dinner, I'll take the entire jewelry box to her. They'll have treasured memories for her."

The china cabinet's upper shelf was packed with German tea cups and saucers, and the lower had orderly sets of Russian matryoshka nesting dolls.

"I'm surprised these are here; maybe imported by a soldier or refugee family."

On the floor she began to unravel the layers, on and on with at least twelve wooden dolls inside, each hand-painted in a white and blue theme of a snow princess, and finely shellacked. The last wouldn't open easily.

"Another doll should be inside, but it's so tightly wedged."

Twisting and turning she heard a rattle. "Something is here."

Her hands gripped tightly in both directions, with her face red and knuckles whitening. At last it breached, and a key on a gold chain fell to the floor. She examined it for a marking or engraving to hint where the key belonged.

I wonder. Perhaps a cabinet, or the grandfather clock, or the safety deposit box that Abel had. Ah, curiosity.

Dusk had fallen on Heidelberg and Rosa realized she was in darkness. As the grandfather clock struck six, she tried the key in the front panel of the tall case.

Click, click. The door sprung open.

At the first inspection, she let her fingers touch the edges of the door frame.

The top portion has a panel that seems inconsistent with the age. It's not matched to the mahogany, and is thick like a pine overlay. Adam will be here soon. I must get ready.

A sudden urge took her to look through Angelina's old clothes, still in the closet. Abel hadn't been bold enough to give them away, and it gave him comfort that her belongings were still intact.

Standing at a mirror in an emerald green dress, she recalled how she felt as a young girl in the 40's, ready for a night on the town. The bodice was lace, and a row of rosebud pearl buttons covered with green silk ran from the neckline to the waist. She pulled her hair into an upsweep using Angelina's alabaster combs.

I'm not sure if Adam would recognize the dress. Maybe it's too forward of me.

With immediate misgivings, she was about to change when Adam knocked at the door.

"Come in, Adam." Rosa heard the latch key turn in the lock and his footsteps in the parlor.

She had begun to notice small things, like his left foot that was heavier than his right. She knew the sounds of him, and a warm feeling rose from her chest up her neck and to her cheeks, with anticipation to see him.

In the parlor, Adam was standing by the fireplace searching for the loose brick.

"Hello, Adam. It isn't there anymore."

From the rosewood cabinet, she took the crumpled paper from the drawer.

"Here it is."

Carefully, he smoothed the brittle creases at the kitchen table. "I hope my translation will present the letter well."

Dear Santa,

I am seven years old and live in Heidelberg. My father died last Christmas and Santa didn't know where I was, so I didn't get anything. I am writing this year to let you know I am staying with my Mom and Granddad over the clock shop in Old Town square.

All I ask is that you bring us a Christmas dinner to share with my sister, aunts and uncles and my cousins. We get hungry and my Mom often doesn't eat. She thinks I don't notice so I will eat, but I do notice.

Grandma Angelina was raised by Jewish parents and I don't understand why so many Germans hate her for that. Please keep Grandmother and Mother safe from the Nazis. There are bad people marching on our town streets wearing uniforms and carrying guns, hurting and stealing our people.

I will be traveling to America soon to stay with my Stanford relatives because they say a terrible war is coming and I may not be safe here much longer.

Be safe when you travel and have a Merry Christmas, Santa.
Signed:
Your friend, Jacob George Stanford

"Your English was excellent. My guess is that the letter was written around the time of that photo of you and Jake in front of Granddad's tree."

"Yes, that's about right. I'd forgotten how hungry we were back then. Jake asked me soon after if I got a St. Nicholas treat in my boot and what it was. I don't even recall what it could have been, but I remember Jake being dejected that perhaps the grand old Christmas gentlemen might not be who we thought."

"How old were you then?"

"Jake was a year younger than me. We were close for quite a while and I felt like I lost my twin when he left for America. I didn't hear from him again because the war was aggressive and folks gave up the ordinary things in life, like writing a letter.

One day after the war, Granddad said he had a letter from Jake. He'd gotten his American citizenship and graduated from a high school in New York. I admit I was jealous.

I did hear that Jake was going to be in Germany with his air force unit and I was very glad to see him . . . that was three years ago."

"Yes, three years," Rosa echoed. "I waited for a letter from the Defense Department, hoping he was taken prisoner and that one day he'd come home. I knew in my heart that Jake was gone." Tears streamed down her cheeks and she had to pause. "And now that it's confirmed, I will treasure my memories of my time with Jake and the blessing of my two wonderful boys."

Adam was staring at her with his mouth open.

"What is it, Adam? You look like you've seen a ghost."

"That's Grandmother's dress!"

"Oh, I'm terribly sorry, Adam. I shouldn't have. I felt a need to get to know your family . . . my family by marriage."

"I've never seen a more beautiful vision. That's even the way she wore her hair. Grandmother Angelina was a beauty for sure, but it is you that is more beautiful."

"Thank you, Adam, but I'd like to change before we go to dinner. You don't want to escort an old lady, do you?"

Adam laughed but watched every step, the way she moved and the swing of her hair, as she went to the bedroom to change.

Minutes later she was ready, in a white silk blouse, burgundy skirt and black patent belt.

Adam held her coat. "Tonight we'll walk along the Neckar canal. The river runs from the Rhine and the Black Forest through all of Heidelberg. You'll enjoy the scenery from the funicular railway."

Rosa was feeling giddy. "Funicular. The name even sounds fun." She laughed. "Tell me more." She had no stress tonight, only joy for these moments that she knew would end too soon.

"We'll travel on the lower railway past the castle to Molkenkur, then the train that inclines at 41% to the highest place in town, the Königsstuhl by the Falconry. A million tourists ride this, taking photos of the town and the castle, the Märchenparadies fairytale children's park and the distant Neckar valley and Rhine lowlands."

"You sound like my own tourist guide."

"Indeed, that I can be." He smiled broadly and she held his arm tighter.

Tourists oohed and aahed as the lower train rolled out past the scenery.

"The castle must be soaked in history," she said. "I imagine stories of war and romance on the bridge. I can almost see the troops marching here, and the victory parade too."

As the car glided up to the last station at Königsstuhl, she raised to her tiptoes for a last glimpse.

"Here we are." Adam took her hand to lead her through the crowd, and when clear of the throng he didn't let go.

"It's barely a block or two. We'll eat at the Zum Roten Ochsen—in English it means the Red Ox Inn. The history spans two hundred years owned by the Spengel family. They know my parents and Granddad, as they came here as long as I remember. My Mother once caught me writing my name on a chair rail, and made me apologize. I feared humiliation, but dear Mrs. Spengel said it was a creative idea, and she wished more children would leave their names for her to remember them."

"How perfectly lovely she is. I can't wait."

The building was pink stucco with quaint stained glass windows and shutters, and an ancient door in mahogany. Mrs. Spengel wore a red, yellow and blue authentic costume with embroidered white aprons over a drindl skirt, and her hair was swirled into braids at the top. She was jolly and exuberant, quite like Rosa had envisioned.

"Adam Armbruster, how rewarding to see you. How are your parents? I haven't seen them for many months. Please remind them that I am still here." Her prattle gave her enough time to sum up the foreigner joining him.

"Pardon my manners, Mrs. Spengel. This is Rosa Stanford, a distant relative from New York."

The reason for the visit suddenly dawned on the hostess. "I'm so sorry; you are here because of your grandfather. He was an admirable man, with kindness and topped with a sense of humor. Heidelberg will not forget such a brave man."

Mrs. Spengel put her hand on Adam's arm, assuring him there would be a fine table for them. "You know I can always find the right space for my special customers." With that, she literally bounced out of sight.

Adam and Rosa were led to the next room through an audience of locals, then greeted by members of a Bavarian oompah band setting up with an accordion, trumpet, tuba, clarinet, trombone, and drums. Patrons were still celebrating Oktoberfest, with noise and laughter at every table.

Rosa cupped her hands at her lips and leaned to Adam. "It's loud here," she shouted. "I love it."

The walls were lined tight with framed glossies of celebrities and notables that had crossed the threshold in the last century. Antique sideboards and ornamental stoves held shelves of stoneware with porcelain beer steins in all sizes. Even the ceiling was an anchor for old antlers and wooden farm implements, salvaged from the Black Forest.

"We passed a photo of my family taken before the war, when we once came to celebrate a birthday. It still hangs in the lobby."

"I want see it on the way out. Please show me."

"They're famous here for their beer selection too. I suggest you try the Schoppen."

She scrunched her nose, but raised her shoulders with a grin to stay polite. "I haven't tasted a beer in years."

"Please try it, even a sip. It will come in a collectable stein with German motifs to take as a souvenir. It is part of the experience of being here."

"Then on your advice I'll try, Adam."

Dinner was delivered on a platter with green salads, a schnitzel with fried potatoes for Rosa, and for Adam a palatine sausage plate with sauerkraut and mashed potatoes.

The band was already ripping through the first set, and although early, Rosa didn't want the evening to ever end. At Adam's suggestion for a dance, she felt like jumping to her feet, but kept her poise as she took his hand.

Any traces of tension she brought from New York were gone as she laughed and swayed, oblivious to the boisterous crowd.

She felt the strength of his hand on her back and closed her eyes knowing she'd been transported into a Cinderella fairytale, dancing with her prince. She whispered her happiness to him and they swirled through another number until the band took its break.

"Well little lady, I should return Cinderella to her castle."
So he thinks I'm Cinderella too, how incredible.

"I'm beginning to believe in magic here. I saw a marvelous confectioner's window on the street. Could we stop on the way back? I'll get a special truffle for your parents. I want to do this, Adam."

The store brimmed with the fragrance of sweets and sugar plums. Fridolin Knösel, the proprietor, was gregarious and rotund, with a compliment for every woman that entered the shop, and witty remarks for the men. Tinsel and decoration lit up the atmosphere, surrounding gingerbread houses, chocolate molds of snowmen, and miniature marzipans of any fruit. In the window was his deluxe Christmas stollen, dusted with icing sugar that resembled fresh snow, with a border of cranberries and holly.

"Hello, Adam. Who is this princess on your arm?"

Knösel turned to Rosa. "Your blue eyes lit up my shop the moment you stepped in my door. Adam is a lucky man."

Rosa delighted in the shopkeeper's words, and giggled like a schoolgirl. "He's not my beau; he's a dear friend showing me the sights of your charming town."

The exchange left them both confused—Adam wishing he were the beau, and Rosa regretting she might have shunned him. She glanced at his face and saw his jaw was tight, and knew her reply had stung him.

She squeezed his arm. "You know you're much more than a tourist guide to me, don't you?"

Adam smiled wistfully and she accepted that as his answer.

The proprietor brought out his chocolate truffle covered marzipan with its pure almond taste. With her approval, he returned with a box, giftwrapped and in a see-through bag adorned with a paper rosette.

At the Brand house, Adam still fought the urge to get on with it and kiss her.

She's my client and my cousin's wife. It could ruin everything during the rest of Rosa's stay. What am I doing?

At the same time, Rosa was gazing into his green eyes. She saw a new twinkle and waited to be swooped into his arms.

What am I thinking? I'm a widow and this is my husband's cousin, but I can't deny that a growing love is burning in my heart. That seems so disrespectful, and he is such a gentleman.

11

Visit to the Armbrusters

On Saturday morning, Rosa waited on a park bench across from the clock store. The cobblestone streets glistened from vehicles splashing through the overnight snow.

She was far away in thought, back in New York, and although she hadn't even been in Heidelberg a week, she knew her life had already changed.

"It's after midnight there and Vivian will have the boys. She's a good mother with her own three, and I know she has activities for Edgar and Will. But I should be at home with my family this time of year."

She frequently glanced across the common. "When Adam gets here, we can wrap up the deal with the clock shop."

She grinned at the thought of the Hansel and Gretel. "But for Mildred, I'll get something else. I wonder what she thinks of a beer stein." At the comical suggestion of Mrs. Fitch drinking beer, she broke into laughter. "Quite preposterous!"

Spotting her, Adam quickened his step. "Good morning, princess." She stepped out to the edge of the curb to meet him.

"And to you, handsome prince." Neither laughed as they shared a moment where words weren't needed. Adam's eyes sparkled, as a child anticipating a wish about to come true.

The sound of Herr Bachmann opening his shop broke the spell, and he welcomed them at the door.

"Good morning, come in . . . come in. Franz will look after any customers while we attend to business."

"Shall we get started then?" Adam suggested.

"Yes. And Rosa, while you're here, you must also come back to my workshop. That's where my elves work. Ha, ha, ha!"

Adam set a tray on the work table with three coffees from the patisserie. Rosa hadn't joined him but stood where the Hansel and Gretel clock had been. The space was empty and her face showed her disappointment.

"Herr Bachmann, did you sell the Hansel and Gretel?"

The clockmaker and Adam exchanged an awkward glance. "Yes, I'm afraid so, Rosa."

Settled around the table, Adam read the documents word for word in German, detailing the offer. Bachmann nodded his approval throughout.

But Rosa's mind wandered as her eyes traveled the length of the room and to the back. The door of the storeroom was open, and she was distracted by the sight of a hanging red cloak and a set of tall stilts.

"That concludes the offer, except one addition. Mrs. Stanford would like a memento, a cuckoo clock to take back."

"Yes, yes, yes . . . I am certainly pleased with the offer, and it is clear to me that you are both kin of Abel Brand. He was a generous soul and brought us many customers that relied on his recommendation. He was a talker with the tourists."

Rosa was still distant, now staring into the creamy swirls of her coffee cup.

"Rosa, I'll gladly demonstrate the movements of our finest clocks. Do you have something in mind?"

She didn't want to accept second best, as her heart was settled. Déjà vu swept her back to the age of six or seven years old. It was a Shirley Temple doll, an adorable creation with golden curly ringlets, in a white dress with red polka dots. Rosa had written about it to Santa, but on Christmas morning the very doll was waiting for her sister. Instead, she received a Raggedy Anne and she bore the fragile heartache of a child.

"Do you mind if I take a look around then?"

Rosa was mildly enamored with a stubby mahogany mantle clock and confirmed her selection to Herr Bachmann's surprise.

"But Rosa, I'm puzzled. I thought it was a cuckoo you wanted."

"No, this is the one."

"Very odd indeed about this. I've enjoyed this clock in my shop for a long time. Every time Abel came down, he went directly to it and took the key from the back to wind it. This is a sign, I'm certain."

"Really?"

"Yes, there was something about it that seemed to speak to Abel. Shall I wrap it, or would you like it shipped home?"

"Shipping sounds better as I wouldn't be able to fit it into my case."

"I'll take care of that, but take the key now so it doesn't get misplaced."

Outside, Rosa thanked Adam for the morning, knowing he had appointments for the day.

"How about shopping while I work?" he said. "And I'll pick you up at six."

"I couldn't say no to that. I haven't shopped for myself for too long . . . you know, with two young children. It's time I bought a new dress, and I can wear it to dinner tonight."

On a narrow street lined with shops, a window display drew her inside. She led the clerk back to the front. "It's that one, the sleek black dress with the sequined bodice." She felt guilty at first for trying it on, but standing tall before the mirror, she imagined presenting herself to Adam and felt relief and assurance that he would be pleased.

The price was in German Marks, and in her Frommer's book she found a currency translation, wincing at the conversion.

But I can afford it now, and I must make a suitable impression on the Armbrusters.

Next door, she added black patent sling backs to the ensemble. The old Alstadt market was vibrant already this early, and at Neideregger's Patisserie, she sipped a slow coffee on the patio, observing shoppers' fervor in anticipation of the holidays, everyone oblivious to others.

With no German knowledge, she still knew from the flyer's bold headlines what was 'on sale', and she skimmed the Antik Toy Shop ads of exquisite hand-painted toys and knickknacks.

Only a few streets over. Looks like the place for treasures for my boys.

Affixed to the walls around the circumference of the shop was a platform with a topography of rural roads, bridges and mountains for a running train set. The engine and cars chugged beside a hand-made road up into a forest, then down to a wee station house with a miniature man waving a flag. Flashing steam lights and whistles brought it to life.

"The boys would be mesmerized."

Another shelf held intricate metal toys with moving parts, and Rosa cranked the crane pulley and turned the tractor's steering wheel imagining Will doing it. Armies of miniature green figurines were stacked in boxes on the floor; on the opposite wall were dollhouses with furniture, and deeper in the store were more Russian nesting dolls. A dollhouse with batteries lit up a chandelier and made the fireplace glow. Finally loaded with parcels, she wound her way home to the Brand house.

At six sharp, Adam arrived with a chauffeured sedan for the drive to the Armbruster's residence on the hillside. Her outfit was complete with Angelina's glistening black hair combs and a ruby pendant encased in tiny diamonds on a gold strand.

I hope Florentine doesn't mind.

"You are so gorgeous, Rosa. My family is excited to finally meet you as I've told them all about you."

"What exactly have you said?"

"That you are everything Jake told us you were."

"I am very grateful to your family for permitting me to participate in the Brand estate. It is humbling to be associated with a family of such a generous reputation and pillars of the community."

At the three-story red brick house, Adam helped Rosa out and carried her package up the walk with the jewelry case by its handle. He handed her the box of sweets.

There was barely a need to knock as Florentine had been watching. Adam's mother had thick blonde hair clipped into a bun, high cheekbones, a button nose and the family's green eyes. She rushed forward to hug Rosa.

"Wilkum, Rosa." Her effort at English moved Rosa.

"Thank you. Adam told me so much about his family that I feel I already know you. You are kind to welcome me into your home." Adam translated and Florentine showed a sweet gentleness in her smile.

"No need to translate Adam; my English is plenty good enough," Florentine admonished.

Bogdan Armbruster stood behind his wife, heavy set with thick, dark curly hair and a burst of grey at his temples. Rosa admired his strong chin, long nose and brown eyes.

Adam has his mother's eyes and compassion, but his father's coloring and humble demeanor.

"Please, Fraulein Armbruster, this is for you." Rosa extended the chocolates and the case with Angelina's jewelry.

"Oh, please, call me Florentine, and thank you so much for thinking of us. We are delighted that you are here; we are all family."

She recognized the jewelry box and with a thank you she relieved Rosa of it without resistance.

"Oh, marzipan. You know Fridolin's is my favorite!"

Coming down the stairs was another man that looked like Adam. He was more extroverted and harder to read.

"This is David. He's my big brother."

David gave the brotherly punch to Adam's shoulder and offered his hand in greeting to Rosa.

"He's teasing you—Adam is the oldest." David was shorter than Adam with lighter brown hair and broad shoulders, and Rosa thought to herself that he would make a perfect St. Nicholas.

A magnificent table was laid out by Florentine with her most important crystal and china that she kept for special occasions. Rosa noted that the table was set for six, not five.

"Please take a chair," Florentine said, and saw Rosa's eyes go the empty spot.

"I hope we don't confuse you, Rosa. You are here because of Abel and I wanted him to know. The chair at the end is for him . . . in spirit at least."

"Such a nice thought."

The feast began with a creamy cucumber salad, then both Bavarian Schnitzel and German sausage, braised red cabbage, and a mash of potatoes, celery root and a touch of turnip. Between courses they rested for conversation.

David kept the wine glasses filled and stopped at Rosa's. "Adam tells us you have made excellent decisions for my grandfather." His English was excellent, and Rosa wondered from his tone whether it was intended as a compliment or resentment. Adam immediately jumped in.

"Everything has been true to Granddad's wishes. David, is there something that you would like from the Brand house before we complete the probate?"

"No, no, Adam . . . we've all been through this before."

"Rosa, I'm a matter of fact guy," David said. "You shouldn't read anything into my words. Granddad made sure that all his grandchildren were provided for before he became ill. I have artwork and old books that I was attached to, and had no need for knickknacks and old clothes. I'm not what you would call sentimental."

"I'm glad," Rosa said, "but of course if there is anything, anything at all that you would like, please come and take it before I leave for New York."

Bogdan asked, "When do you go back?"

"I'll book the 22nd so I'm home for Christmas with my boys."

"Of course, family should be together at Christmas," Florentine agreed.

"This is the first time I've been away from my children since they were babies. It was not easy to pick up and leave so quickly with so much ambiguity ahead of me. However, I have other relatives in New York, and we've adopted a grandmother in our apartment building. Without them, I couldn't have come to Heidelberg."

From the corner of her eye, Rosa noticed Adam fidgeting with the unused cutlery, and perhaps avoiding looking at her. The table became quiet, and she knew him well enough to see his stress.

Florentine sensed the conversation was going the wrong way and rose for dessert. She returned with a three-layer chocolate cake, thick with butter cream icing, and came back again with a rich poppy seed one decorated with strawberries.

"Which would you choose, Rosa?" Bogdan asked, holding a silver cake knife, and Adam intervened.

"My Mom makes the best chocolate cake in the world."

"Chocolate cake, please."

Rosa insisted on clearing the table with Adam's mother, for moments to talk to know each other better. Rosa tried a few German words that Adam had taught her, and Florentine compensated with fine broken English.

"Sorry about your husband, Rosa. I remember Jake as a young boy. He was much like his mother and grandmother. And Adam and Jake were tight as cousins; if one had a sleepover at Abel's, the other pleaded to be there too."

Rosa envisioned the tender memory. "Thank you. I really lost him three years ago, and I wasn't aware until Adam told me the recent circumstances. It must have been unbearable being tortured and living in a prison camp . . ." Rosa held her pain in abeyance, and felt it best not to say more.

"Bless you. I'm glad you have family support in New York."

"There are cousins, and of course my children. But I'll admit it's been difficult on my own. The youngest is four and I leave him with a sitter much of the time. I always thought in the back of my mind that Jake would return one day. At least now, I can go forward with my life."

"You're a good woman, Rosa. In time your heart will belong to another."

"Yes . . . in time."

"Adam mentioned the memorial service for Abel and Jake. I've booked the Providence church for Tuesday afternoon, and the priest will announce it in the Sunday bulletin. Our church ladies group insist on providing a lunch reception."

"Thank you so much for looking after this."

Florentine was biting her lip to say more.

"If I may, Rosa . . ."

"Of course, you can say whatever you like to me."

"Tonight, I see my Adam has become invested in you. You must relate to how a mother can see into her child's soul, like an open window."

"I do understand."

"Adam has had a difficult life. He was different after the war, then poor Astrid died and it seemed like he gave up. He has not yet had a lot of happiness in his life. I wished I could ease his pain, but that must come from inside."

"Yes, I know the kind of pain you talk of."

"There is something new in his eyes, Rosa, when he looks at you and when he talks about you. You have given him back some lost life. I would do anything to spare him pain."

"Aunt Florentine! Do you fear that I will cause Adam pain?"

Rosa brushed a tear aside to continue. "That's impossible. Adam is my dearest friend in Heidelberg, my encourager, my strength, but above all a respectable gentleman."

Florentine embraced Rosa with a gentle hug. She knew Rosa didn't see from her own heart what was happening. However, Florentine was a woman in charge of her family and sensed a fear deep inside, that her influence with Adam had waned since Astrid's death. Now Rosa presented a situation she wasn't sure how to deal with.

Rosa found Adam in the living room talking with his father about the political affairs of Germany. When she appeared in the doorway, his face brightened. She wanted to be near him but her feet felt like lead and she stood instead, waiting.

Adam has feelings for me.

She was neither shocked nor unnerved, it was peculiarly comforting. Florentine strutted into the parlor. "Come along everyone, we can't be late for the evening church service."

Neither Bogdan nor Adam's vehicle had room for everyone, and Adam called for the chauffeur to bring the second sedan around, and they were alone again.

Rosa was still edgy, with the turmoil from Florentine's words.

"Are you alright, Rosa?"

"Of course. Your family is wonderful, and I had forgotten what that was like."

"I know when you are not being truthful, Rosa. Something is bothering you."

She sat silently and his hand reached to hers. "My mother can be blunt sometimes. Did she say something to upset you?"

Rosa didn't answer, but turned away as her eyes began to sting and a slight shudder ran through her body.

"Everything will sort itself out, Rosa."

"I'm feeling overwhelmed, Adam . . . I'm glad we can be alone for a bit."

The Providence Church was packed to the doors with music enthusiasts to hear Bach's B Minor Mass. A line spilled outside, wanting a pew for the concert. Florentine arrived early and stood at the double doors waiting for Adam and Rosa.

Reaching for Adam's sleeve, Florentine whispered, "Your father and David are holding seats. We are regulars here. Squeeze past the lineup. We always have our own reserved pew." Her whisper became intentionally loud so newcomers would see she was privileged and let them pass.

The seating was jammed too tight for Florentine's pleasure, but Rosa and Adam were happy to squeeze.

"The music is inspiring, Adam. I've never heard Bach before; I'll make a more concerted effort to attend classical music back in New York. The Christmas Eve pageant at St. Mary's is the best I've had in my schedule."

"St. Mary's Christmas Eve. I am imagining it," Adam said.

A prayer preceded a benediction and soon the crowd milled in conversation toward the exits.

12

Impossible Worlds Divide

*A*dam didn't pursue their planned trip to Zum Ritter's, but instead asked the taxi to return to Abel's house directly after the Lutheran service. His troubled emotions had been visible through the evening, and Rosa didn't encouraged him otherwise, or help to ease his torment.

"This evening has been quite eventful, Rosa. Perhaps we should enjoy the Zum Ritter another evening. There has been a lot to take in for one day."

Rosa was mildly disheartened as she had passed the old world charm of the hotel during her shopping excursion and anticipated a romantic evening with 16th century renaissance frescoes and cultural music, as Adam had described.

"I see . . . whatever you think is best, Adam." She tightened her lips, not to show disappointment.

"Would you like me to keep you company for a bit, or would you prefer to be alone, Rosa?"

"My apologies for being rude, Adam. I don't want to be alone right now, if it's not an imposition."

"Shall I make a pot of tea?" he offered.

She squinted and grinned. "Does Abel keep any brandy in the house?"

Adam pulled her close. "Was it that bad?" Evoking laughter, he sighed a breath of relief.

"No it wasn't. Sometimes the truth is hard to deny. Life isn't always easy, but a wise man told me recently that everything sorts itself out in time."

He unlocked a parlor cabinet and slid out a shelf with an assortment of comforts.

"What's your pleasure, Ma'am?"

"Courvoisier?" Rosa opened the glass china cabinet for two short-stemmed crystal snifters, and laid out her tray of confections on the table.

"For a simple girl from New York, you have refined taste in cognac," Adam said.

After a sip, Rosa remembered about the closet.

"Adam, since you're here, I want to show you something."

He followed her to the bedroom closet. The floor was now clear of shoes and it was apparent something was behind the exposed wooden panel.

"What happened here?"

"After I packed up, I saw a bit of that material."

Rosa was now sitting on her knees with a snifter in one hand, watching him. Adam tapped on the baseboard and they both listened in silence, then heard a distinct click.

Peering into the opening, Adam recoiled. "By gosh, Rosa, I know what this is."

He paced the room, scratching his chin and his head.

"Please go on," she said. "I might as well tell you now that I have the type of curiosity that killed the cat."

Adam looked completely baffled by her comment. Rosa laughed at his reaction and tried to explain. "My curiosity doesn't let me give up too easily."

At first Adam was agitated with the discovery, as old memories flooded back. He knew where this exposure would lead and insisted on calling an acquaintance from the Museum who specialized in wartime artifacts. Thumbing through the white pages, he dialed and was about to hang up when a voice answered.

"Ivan? It's Adam Armbruster."

Rosa left for the kitchen and didn't hear Adam's muffled conversation with his counterpart.

Finding her at the kitchen table with her brandy, he sighed. "We'll wait for the professionals so we don't taint history. A team will come to investigate first thing in the morning."

"I can sleep in the spare room tonight. The master bedroom now seems a bit crowded," she offered.

"Are you sure? I can book you back at a hotel if you prefer."

"Of course not, I am perfectly fine here."

Preoccupied, Adam took the last gulp of brandy in his glass. "I'll see you in the morning then."

His goodnight did not have its usual warmth, and Rosa felt empty for the first time in Heidelberg. From the window she watched as he disappeared toward Alstadt.

It suddenly occurred to her that the tall case was ticking particularly loud tonight, reverberating into her thoughts.

Time, indeed time goes much too quickly. If I only had a glimpse of the past and the future, today would be so much easier.

The moon cast enough light through the second bedroom window to keep her awake, reflecting on the day. Her ears were tuned to the tapping from below, and as the rhythm became melodic, she drifted to sleep.

It was still dark when Rosa opened her eyes, and she sat upright. "There is much to do today and no time to waste."

She raised the window to inhale the cold morning air, and watched the early street activity of merchants preparing for the day. She turned to the dressing table to brush her hair.

"Look at me, a widow with a frown over my brow, the corners of my lips downturned with regret. I'll not stand for that."

Finding a smock of Angelina's, she covered her dress and tied her hair up in a kerchief to protect against dust.

Sipping on hot tea and nibbling on a biscuit, she listened for the sound of Adam's steps on the stairs. By the time the tea was cold, her mind had journeyed to what it might have been like to have been under the oppression in the war—what Angelina must have felt when soldiers marched up these stairs to take her and her daughter away to a horrid place where she might never return.

"It's unfathomable to comprehend such atrocities. I'm glad I came to Germany . . . it strengthens me to have such pride that my Jake gave his life for the freedom of his own people. Dear Jake, there will always be a place for you in my heart, and I confess that your cousin is now making a spot of his own."

Whether it was a sign or a reaction to the door downstairs, one of the nested teacups in the china cabinet fell from its rack and crashed on the shelf below.

Rosa gasped and was on her feet. "Is that you, Jake?"

The key turned in the lock.

"What's the matter, Rosa? You're white as a ghost?"

Adam helped her up from her knees as she scooped the broken glass into a dustpan.

"I was having a chat with Jake . . . then this!"

"I'll make you a strong coffee, Rosa. We need to talk about Jake."

At the table, she rested her head on her clasped hands, listening for the percolator to sing.

"Thanks, Adam. I don't know how I'd get through all this without you."

He nodded and took the chair across. His brow furrowed and as she observed new dark bags under his eyes, she noticed grey strands of hair over his right temple, too premature for his age.

"About the memorial service at the church tomorrow . . ." In mid-sentence, he was interrupted by a knock at the door. "That must be Ivan."

At the door, Ivan Atkinson was beaming about the discovery. Behind him were two workmen in overalls, one with a wooden box of intricate tools. Atkinson was lanky, with distinguished gold rim spectacles halfway down his nose, and he presented an immediate air of self-confidence

"I was most pleased about your possible finding, Adam. It isn't often we recover the old escape routes still intact almost twenty-five years later."

Atkinson's eyes shifted to Rosa.

"Pardon me, Ivan. This is my cousin's wife, Rosa Stanford. She's visiting from New York. In fact, it was Rosa that found the canvas threads in the closet."

Rosa offered her hand. "It is a pleasure to meet you Ivan."

After a firm grip, he produced a business card with official embossing, Kurpfälzisches Museum der Stadt Heidelberg, Supervisor of Historical Artifacts.

"My honor, Rosa. Please share what you found."

"They were shreds of canvas through a crack in the wall seam. Adam has described how Germans and Jews feared being sent to concentration camps, and in haste some preserved their valued art in caches. I wondered if this were such a thing."

Adam added. "When I was a child, my grandfather defended his neighbors and friends who received registration orders and were forced to wear white arm bands identifying themselves as Jews. It was this way throughout Germany."

"It's likely that this has been boarded up since about 1942," Ivan conjectured.

"Yes, about that time," Adam said. "Abel smuggled refugees into his apartment using disguises and many times in the dark of night. My grandmother always had a hot meal waiting, then provided warm clothing and a sack of dry biscuits from her rations, and candles and matches to help them on their way into the Black Forest. They always left hopeful of safety somewhere beyond.

"One at a time, they disappeared through the back of this closet. I found out later that a long wooden ladder goes to the roof, to a trap door under a patch of tile beside the shack on the upper terrace. One day, my brother David, my cousin

Jake, and I were caught by Granddad for climbing up the shaft. He gave us a sack of biscuits as the refugees would have, and made us sleep overnight in the ladder compartment in the dark to see what it was like. Sure sobered us up."

"No doubt there would be others on the roof that helped them onwards through escape routes on their treks to the forest," Atkinson surmised.

"The closet panel hasn't been reopened in all these years. You can see by the age of the wood and nails," Adam said.

Ivan was itching to start. "We'll proceed with caution to preserve their footsteps. The ladder will likely have wood rot."

Atkinson gestured for a helper to pry the panel open but Adam halted him. "No need to pry . . . just press this worn spot on the baseboard and it will open. It's on spring hinges."

With a foot tap, the panel popped open, and a large roll of canvases was visible in the darkness.

Ivan eased them into the light. "Gracious, Adam. These are original pieces of lost art. We learned after the war that many hid their treasures fearing confiscation. This collection alone appears to be between fifteen and eighteen pieces. After the war, a Reclamation Project was set up to match refugees with lost art. I'll send photos with close-ups, and with luck we can get a few matches."

With the first compartment emptied, one workman entered the shaft with a lantern, and the other went to the roof to locate the trap door.

From the bedroom floor, Rosa watched the undertakings, then moved closer to Adam and slipped her arm into his.

"Again I'm sorry for what you and your family have been through." She angled her head to his shoulder.

The first man called out to Atkinson. "A metal box is tucked in the wall on a bit of a shelf. I'm handing it through."

Ivan reached in with special gloves.

"Do you recognize this, Adam?"

"Yes . . . yes I do. You see, Angelina came from Jewish parents and Abel did whatever he could to conceal that. My guess is that you'll find documentation of Angelina's ancestry and Jewish bloodline. If they'd been found, it would have meant certain death to Grandmother."

Suddenly a beam of daylight shone through the shaft from the sky.

"Ahoy below!"

Atkinson stepped into the shaft and could make out his workman on the roof.

"With the forensic kit, take fingerprints from around the inside and outside of the door."

From a cubby hole, the man inside produced some diaries and pouches of jewelry, and Atkinson itemized and labeled every fragment brought out.

"Adam, what is to become of this place now that Abel is gone?" he asked.

"How long do you need for your excavations?"

"We'll take measurements and photos at every step—so it could be several weeks. This is like a historical museum, a rare opportunity to be preserved. It seems there is a piece of history from every traveler that came this way."

Adam hesitated and looked toward Rosa.

"Rosa is living here for the time being. She plans to return to New York on the 22nd. Beyond that we have not yet come to an agreement for the apartment."

He knew Rosa was troubled and followed her to the parlor where she stood to observe the street below.

"What do you think of the idea of making this the Abel Brand Historic House?" she said.

"Tell me more, Rosa."

"I have a vision of it. Everything is still in place, pretty much as it was when Abel returned after the war. Now that I know about the underground movement through this house, I feel that it belongs to the ghosts of victims past. If the museum would like to take it over and preserve the escape tunnel, perhaps they could cover expenses from admission incomes. I had talked to your mother about the rest of the Brand items such as china and furniture, and she suggested we host a charity auction after the funeral tomorrow. Instead, it should stay here where it belongs. Abel, Jake, Angelina, Eve and also future generations can visit whenever they want."

She still hadn't turned to face Adam, but knew how close he was standing.

"Rosa, you have been sent here as Heidelberg's Christmas Angel."

"It's very kind of you to say that, Adam." She turned to him. "I am the fortunate one here, I have a family that I will treasure forever and I've now had the privilege of peeking into the window of the past and to feel their hearts beat."

With anguish he whispered, "I do dread the day you will leave me, Rosa."

She wanted to promise she wouldn't leave and that she wanted to feel safe and secure in his arms, but that was an impossibility.

Not now . . . not ever.

13

December 16, 1962, Memorial Service

osa was accustomed to the chimes of the town church bells ringing, but this day was different. It was Tuesday, the day of the memorial service at Providence Church. She had suggested that Adam not come for her in the morning as she needed time alone with her thoughts and was looking forward to the walk.

Convincing herself that a bit of distance between them might be best under the circumstances, she mocked herself. "The circumstances . . . are that I am a new widow and have these intense feelings for another man."

She didn't fuss to clean, as Atkinson and his crew wouldn't be back today, respecting the service.

Her clothes were ready the night before, and now in a hurry she dressed in her conservative black wool dress and matching hat, and adjusted its thin drop-down veil to cover her forehead. In the mirror, she was satisfied with her modest winter coat, and tucked her black suede gloves in the pockets. As she left the Brand house, she overflowed with emotion.

The mere thought of the house as a war memorial thrilled Bogdan and Florentine, and right away she called off the ladies' charity auction, and still managed to stay at the center of attention in her announcement. She wore a mid-length black pleated skirt, a frilly white blouse and fitted crepe jacket. Her hat was midway between flamboyant and respectable and she clearly would not go unnoticed.

At the chapel's front row, the Armbrusters held reserved seats, and Adam kept watching the back of the vestibule for Rosa. A fluster in the hallway caught his eye.

A unit of three soldiers had entered in full military dress and were now in the crowd. Adam recognized one as the man he had interviewed, who responded to his ad for anyone knowing the whereabouts of Jacob Stanford.

"That's Moretti!"

Adam left his seat and went to the back to make introductions. A Commander Robinson saluted to Adam, then the two airmen.

"I trust we are not intruding, Herr Armbruster. My veteran, Vincenzo Moretti, saw an announcement of this memorial service. It is the honor of the United States Veterans Defense Department to participate if we may. We had not received a formal request to be represented, but we are comrades and proud to have served with Captain Stanford."

At that moment, Rosa walked through the main door and stopped dead in her tracks, seeing the uniforms. Adam moved to her and offered his arm for support.

"Rosa, these are Jake's friends from the Ramstein military base. They have come to pay their respects. Will that be alright with you?"

"Commander Wayne Robinson, Ma'am." The first saluted and took a military stance, then the others.

"Private Vincenzo Moretti. Prisoner of war with Captain Jacob Stanford, Ma'am." He stepped back.

"Airman Richard Wenchel. I was the Captain's gunner the day we were hit, Mrs. Stanford, Ma'am." Weasel followed the salute of his mates.

"Thank you for coming," she said. "This means a great deal." With authority she turned to Adam. "Can you arrange for seating at the front for our friends?"

"Certainly, Rosa. You go on, there are two seats by the aisle next to my parents. Go ahead and get settled."

The walk to the front row seemed so far away. Rosa's feet had barely moved in the aisle when Adam noticed her begin to waver. He rushed and caught her as her knees buckled, and a church page was there in seconds with a glass of water.

"Don't worry," Adam said, "I'll carry you to a bench in the outer foyer to get composed in private."

"I can walk, really. With your support, we'll continue."

Adam's arm was around her waist as they walked. Florentine turned to see what was causing the delay and was disconcerted to see her son helping his cousin's wife in such a familiar manner.

Rosa eased into the seat beside her. "I'll be right back," Adam whispered.

Florentine struggled with the circumstances. The thought had never occurred to her of a fainting episode to send her family into a tailspin.

Instead of consoling the grieving widow, she whispered into Rosa's ear, "Sit up straight and get a grip on yourself, dear. Appearances are important."

Confused by Florentine's rebuke, she waited for Adam's return, determined not to be intimidated by his mother. The episode in fact fortified her and she sat taller and looked toward the Lutheran Minister at the front who had observed the exchange. He nodded his head slightly with a compassionate smile.

When the congregation was full, the brief military contingent marched in symmetry to the row across the aisle, and turned to salute the family before taking their seats.

Rosa whispered, "Aunt Florentine, these men are Jake's Ramstein unit. It was so kind of them to come and pay their respects today."

"Yes. Very nice, dear."

Florentine released a slow, silent breath, and her shoulders relaxed, enjoying the words 'Aunt Florentine'.

The church was jammed to the back with standing in the foyer, as Abel had spent his life in Heidelberg and earned his reputation, heralded by the community.

News of Jake's heroic efforts to assist East Germans escape from the Berlin Wall had well run its course but the legends continued to circulate and were on everyone's lips today.

A church bulletin gave tribute to both men and highlighted Jake's tours of duty and heroism. It was said that he gave his life to spare his mates, knowing he would not be rescued.

The pipe organ accompanied singers in *Almighty God* and *The Battle Hymn of the Republic*. Bogdan Armbruster read a eulogy for Abel Brand that touched many from the town, then Vincenzo Moretti spoke about his friend and co-pilot, and of Jake's heroism in his last moments.

The chapel became silent for the Lutheran Minister. "I now call on Adam Armbruster, one of Abel's grandsons."

Rosa's heart pumped with pride that she could be here.

Adam was eloquent. "These are two great men with a common bloodline. Each was prepared to die to save the other. I am overcome with the bravery of both my grandfather and my cousin to forge into enemy territory to save their own and many unknown victims of the wars. We are still fighting a war to free our East German comrades from the tyranny of the Soviets.

"Abel's wife, Angelina, and his daughter, Eveline, both died in concentration camps. Unfortunately, my dear mother is the only child of the Brand family to survive. She has been courageous and generous as we have invited Rosa, Jake's widow, into our family. Rosa Stanford, has two young boys back in New York who have lost their father and we all grieve for them too. Jake served in both the Second World War and the Korean, then as a pilot in Ramstein right here in Germany.

"Three years ago, he was near the end of his tour of duty and his return to America. But fate had other plans, and the Dresden 152 was shot down—the three men on board were first presumed dead. We are honored to have with us his two airmen who were with him on that dreadful flight—Officer Vincenzo Moretti and Officer Richard Wenchel."

Adam's voice cracked as Rosa's tears gathered in her eyes.

"Prior to that, three years ago, I was privileged to go with Jake to Granddad's house here for a visit. We were like small boys again, delighting in his stories and affection. Abel insisted that Jake should return to Heidelberg with his family—and so he has."

The room hushed again when Commander Robinson was called to perform his military duty on behalf of the Veterans Department, with Jake's airmen by his side. The American flag was draped over an empty coffin and folded into a triangle, then the Commander marched to Rosa's seat and presented it.

Grasping it to her bosom, she closed her eyes tight enough to hold back the sudden wave of grief. Adam rested his hand on hers, and gave her a squeeze of reassurance. With many eyes on them, he whispered quietly, "I'm here for you, Rosa."

Officer Moretti remained standing and raised his trumpet to play *The Last Post*. As it echoed though the chapel, tears flowed and many stood in respect to Abel and Jake, and in memory of other lost family members and soldiers, and for souls still missing.

With a closing prayer the service concluded, and the family greeted well-wishers at a receiving line in the basement before the luncheon. Rosa was eager to talk with Moretti and Weasel to know about their time with Jake.

"It was indeed kind that you came today, gentlemen."

Moretti said, "It was my wife Hilda . . . her family lives in Heidelberg, and she saw the newspaper posting. She knew that I often talked about Jake and Weasel. Of course when I heard, I had to be here."

Vince was uneasy, fumbling in his pocket. "Rosa, I have something for you."

In his hand were Jake's dog tags, and she touched them with the tips of her fingers. Then from his breast pocket he took out a tattered picture.

"Jake had this with him on his last mission. I thought you'd like to have it back—it was recovered from the wreckage. He kissed this picture of his family before take-off on all our assignments."

"Oh, no! Were you with him in his last moments?"

"During the downing of the plane we were separated, but two years ago while I was a held prisoner in East Germany, we met again. There was always a plan of escape being calculated, and when we had it down to the moment, we organized to go under a cover of darkness. Jake had smuggled a message to his grandfather who waited with a vehicle on the west side. Most of our convoy made it under the barb wire, but Jake held back for the last one to clear. We heard rapid gunfire from the tree line. Jake insisted on being a decoy and agreed to meet us. I turned back and there wasn't a chance. He was crawling on his knees, but there was more fire. I'm certain he was taken quickly and didn't suffer."

"Thank you, Moretti. I needed to hear that. I have waited three years for him to come home, and the Veterans Affairs department waffled about whether he was killed or not. I guess they were right."

Rosa pondered opening an invitation to Moretti, to glean more details about Jake's demise, but instead opted to accept the finality of their meeting. She had come to terms that today was her official good-bye to Jake, although he would forever hold a piece of her heart.

Lively chatter of parishioners and curious townsfolk had taken over in the basement hall. Rosa recognized the Spengels, Herr Bachmann and Franz, Ivan Atkinson, Fridolin Knösel, the Antik Toys clerk and even the oompah tuba player. Many nameless faces she had only seen in town offered condolences, including tenants from Abel's building. Few had memories of Jake, but everyone had a story about the genial old man.

Adam saw her through the crowd standing alone and knew she was dealing with anxiety. He broke away and returned to her side, and she heaved a sigh of relief to be with him.

"Are you alright, Rosa?"

"Yes, and today I have come to the end of a page."

"Mother asked us back to the house tonight for dinner." He waited and watched her eyes. "But I know that today was a momentous event and you might want to rest."

"You should be with your family, Adam. I'll be fine at Abel's."

"Yes . . . and so will I."

"Adam, your mother lost her father all over again and needs assurance. I would never come between you and your family."

"Mother will have many dinners to come. You only have a few more days in Heidelberg. If you are trying to get rid of me, say so. But as you say you're curious like a cat, I am stubborn like an ox."

Rosa's face changed to her broadest smile, at last able to be amused.

"I could never want to get rid of you, Adam." Rosa thought if she said more she would stutter and blubber.

"Then it's settled. A Gasthaus close to the apartment can package hot dinners in boxes and I'll bring a bottle of wine. I'll take you home first, then I'll be back by seven."

Returning to Abel's, she walked immediately to the Lufthansa office.

"I have a return ticket to New York and wish to reserve a seat on December 22nd to LaGuardia."

"From Frankfurt then?"

"Yes I'll take the train."

"Here you are, Ma'am. "You need to call twenty-four hours before your flight to reconfirm."

Rosa examined the ticket in sober thought. "Yes, I'll do that. Is there a telegraph office nearby?"

14

December 17, 1962. Tying up the Brand Estate

Wednesday morning was crisp with a new dust of snow washing the cobblestone. Rosa raised the front window to inhale the cool air and take in the Christmas spirit she could see below in this quaint town she was calling home.

Ivan Atkinson's workmen arrived at the Brand house at 9:00 a.m. Rosa welcomed them and showed him a spare key to be used when needed. She praised him for their progress, and he described upcoming visits by a museum photographer and a radio station interested in a documentary of Abel's life.

With the morning activity starting up, she was glad to step out into the courtyard. Going down the staircase, she stopped to listen to tapping, the same melodic rhythm she'd heard a few nights earlier.

Must be Mr. Bachmann in his workshop.

With a brisk walk to Market Square, she wired a telegram to Vivian and Mildred with her return travel plans, a mental confirmation that her time in Heidelberg was coming to an end. She struggled with the dilemma but had no solution.

Adam was tied up for the morning with paperwork for the sale and lease of the apartments, and he'd meet her for lunch. There was still much to do yet to formalize agreements and arrange for a trust in New York for the Stanford family.

She felt at home now on the Haupstrasse, the shopping avenue and center of Altstadt, and for the first time she found herself greeting strangers as she walked toward the Heidelberg Castle.

At Wohlfahrt's Christmas store, she mulled over the kunsthandwerk souvenirs and Christmas treasures, and handpicked a selection of specialties and chocolate Santas to be boxed, along with carved wooden trinkets wrapped in tissue.

At the square's center, the skating rink was filled with families, and Rosa couldn't help but think about Edgar and Will at home.

This is their favorite time of year. I should be there with them.

Close to the bridge was a wooden Bavarian house decked in red and green, with a sleigh on the roof. Over the door hung the welcoming sign 'North Pole', and Rosa's curiosity led her inside to find the grand old man called Santa Claus in the center hall. He was seated as if he were holding court, with children whispering desires and adoration into his ear, and the more mischievous ones daring a tug on his bushy beard.

"Ho, ho, ho. Now you be a good boy. I do believe you are on the 'Nice' list."

Rosa stood by the Christmas tree, observing the faces of the children as they raced to their parents, telling of his whiskers and his admonition to leave sugar cookies and milk, and carrots for his reindeer.

The longer she looked, the more her imagination took flight.

I wonder if that's Ludwig Bachmann . . . the red cloak is strikingly similar to the one hanging in his back shop. Double duty as clockmaker and Santa Claus, what an incredible man.

Reminiscing, she envisioned Will insisting on sleeping under the tree last year, with hopes of seeing Father Christmas sneak into their apartment to fill their stockings. As hard as he tried to be awake for it, the slumber fairy had her way and he was soon asleep.

And my sensible Edgar. He didn't think I'd notice that he was trying to sleep with one eye open waiting for signs of an elf or sounds of reindeer on the roof. I sure miss them.

Rosa found a park bench to read a Christmas brochure of the significance of decorations of the Tree of Knowledge, a tradition from the 16th century. Looking up at the skating rink, her eyes were taken with the magnificence of the Christmas tree on the center island, with brilliant lights gifted from Venice's City Hall, and dried fruits, flowers and roasted nuts as decorations.

"Oh my goodness, I am to meet Adam at Scharffs Schlossweinstube on the Schlosshof. I'd better hurry." The words were hard for her, and she laughed and said them again.

Adam was outside and saw her scurrying his way with parcels under each arm. Rosa was impressed with the elegance of the dusty pink dining room with its high back padded purple chairs. She ran her hand over the crisp linen tablecloth.

"This is lovely, Adam."

"I hope your morning was festive, Rosa. I want you to enjoy what we have." He set a portfolio case on the empty chair. "I brought more documents to sign and by tomorrow I should have the rest."

"I didn't realize how many events are scheduled for Christmas. My vocabulary is slightly better every day, and I read on a post that each of the Thursdays preceding Christmas is called 'Klöpfelnächte'. Did I say that right?"

"Klöpfelnächte—but more of a 'k' sound that a 'ch'."

"I'll work on that," she laughed.

"And yes, tomorrow night is the custom where children in folk costumes and dressed as shepherds go knocking door to door. When the homeowner answers, their sweet soprano voices sing carols and hymns, meant to bestow blessings for their kindness. In return, they carry small urns to collect change for charity. We'll pick up coins at the bank for tomorrow."

"Bless their young hearts. Adam, I love it here, but you know I do miss my boys."

"You've promised to show me more photos. Hearing about them, I'm guessing that Edgar is like you and Will is more like Jake. Am I right?"

"You are indeed a good listener." Rosa dug into her handbag for a plastic envelope with snapshots from home.

"They're fine looking lads, Rosa. Do they know of their German heritage?"

"Everything happened so quickly, I didn't want them to worry, so I thought I'd explain when I get home. By the way, I made my reservation for the 22nd."

"Yes . . . the 22nd." Adam deferred to his menu so he wouldn't say anything he'd regret.

"We will be finished by then, won't we?"

"The estate documents, yes. But I may ask you to sign a Power of Attorney should anything else come up . . . unless you want to come back again." Her face glowed with his tease.

"If you let me order, Rosa, its time you tried our favorite Heidelberg meal . . . fried carp. I must explain that grown men spend weekends going to the mountain's rivers to hunt carp. Yes, carp is a fish, but a flying one. They come to the marshes and bulrushes to feed, then leap in the air, and hunters use bows and arrows to shoot them in mid-flight. They're bigger than American Salmon, with heavy rugged scales like an armadillo. But don't worry, it's served lean and clean, fried in butter."

"Bigger than a salmon," she repeated.

"This big." He stretched his arms out full length.

"And have you caught one?"

"When I was a boy, yes. With Granddad."

After lunch, Adam brought out a raft of papers. "There's the two sales on the second floor to the existing tenants . . . both couples send their gratitude to you. Next is a year-to-year lease for the student unit, with automatic renewal if they choose. The next is much longer, but it concludes the sale of Abel's partnership with Ludwig Bachmann. The clockmaker insists you come into the shop again before you leave, so he can thank you in person."

"Of course, Adam. Let's not leave any stone unturned."

"You say the darnedest things, Rosa."

"It's an American habit. I'll try to be more literal."

"No, don't change anything. I enjoy the learning experience. I need to be in my office this afternoon, as I'm mid-way on agreements with the University to operate Abel's residence as a museum under their authority. Would it be an imposition if I asked you to list the items to remain in the apartment?"

"Gracious no, I'd be doing something useful to help with all this work."

"Thank you. I brought sheets for itemizing. Now no more business. Would you come skating again tonight? It will be a clear night to see the stars, and the moon will be full."

"Adam Armbruster, you are a genius mind reader."

"The Old Town will be illuminated, with Christmas carols piped to the streets. We'll take time in the market and have a hot bratwurst and sauerkraut at one of the carts."

"It will be perfect, Adam."

Scurrying back to the apartment, her attention was drawn to her image in the window of one of the shops.

You could do better, Rosa. Perhaps a little makeup and don't forget the lipstick. Today is a new day in your life. Perhaps love isn't so very far away again after all.

At the Apotheke, she made her purchases and continued. The workers had gone, and she spread the inventory sheets on the table to begin a list, starting with furniture. In detail, she described items from the war period: the table top radio, enamelware, old boots and shoes, and Angelina's dresser set and lanterns. She hung some of Abel and Angelina's clothing in the closet, and bundled other things for charity.

The apartment looks like someone is coming back someday.

She folded one of Angelina's work smocks for herself and a burgundy hat, then the mid-calf navy blue coat with rabbit fur trim and a matching muff. She needed a new valise to get it to New York, and solved it with a pullman from the charity pile.

Even before Adam came, voices started outside her door. She opened to a collection of small shepherds singing *Stille Nachte*, in broad toothy smiles and hearty spirits. She hummed to start, then joined with English words of *Silent Night*, stopping only to ponder the line, 'All is calm, all is bright'.

"Wait, shepherds! I have coins for you."

Grabbing loose coins from her handbag, she giggled as each dropped into the brass kettle. "Frohe Weihnachten, Fraulein," the group chorused in unison, then tromped down the staircase leaving wet footprints.

Just like home.

15

The Castle, Heidelberg

Rosa had pretty much taken over Abel's armchair for the comfort, but also to appreciate his view to the street below. With dusk, the shadow of lanterns on posts filtered over the stone surface, energizing her spirit of romance. When Adam came through the door, she was dressed in the fur trimmed long coat, her red scarf and leather gloves.

"Shall we go, Fraulein?" he teased.

"Can we go to the Heidelberg Castle?" She surprised herself at her sudden enthusiasm. "I read that the Twelve Days of Christmas are being celebrated with a display of Art-Advent."

"Yes, we shall go to the palace courtyard," he said. "Near the skating rink in the shadow of the castle, we'll pass hundreds of wooden huts, where you'll see the best of craftsmanship."

With no demand on their time, they sauntered with her arm snug in his. She tugged on his hand to stop at the Zum Heiriten Christkindl carousel. Rosa's eyes lit up and Adam knew she was lost in a memory. It was a time she took Edgar to the amusement park and boardwalk at Coney Island, on the last Christmas Jake was home before shipping to Germany.

"Here, Rosa, we're going to take a spin. I'll help you up if you pick the horse you want." The collector took his change, and Adam lifted her side-saddle onto a pink and blue horse and jumped on the adjacent one as the music began.

With the carousel whirling, she turned to him. "I don't want to do this anymore, Adam."

He moved closer to help her down. "We have to wait for it to come to a stop. Are you not well?"

She grabbed the lapel of his coat and pulled closer putting her head on his shoulder. She could feel his strength and his heart beat. "That's not what I mean."

Back on steady ground, Adam was puzzled. "I'm sorry, I shouldn't have presumed that you would enjoy the carousel."

"That's *not* what I meant."

She looked up at him with adoration admiring his strong jaw, his kind eyes and the gentle soul he was protecting. He pulled her closer without saying a word and felt her cling. This was a feeling he'd never had before.

With hands tight, they walked across the sandstone Prince Elector Carl Theodor Bridge spanning the Neckar River and leading to the castle, on the north flank of Königsstuhl hill.

They were still torn with emotion and respective pain and she was glad when Adam broke the ice.

"Did you know that on this very bridge on April 1st, 1945, the Germans surrendered to the 10th Armored Division of the US, carrying a white flag? I won't forget the day of celebration when West Germany was finally freed. All Germans will remember it forever. I was a lucky one, Rosa. My parents survived and we were able to recover our home in relatively good repair."

"Too much blood was lost in the war," she said. "I'm sorry you lived through such fear."

"I better appreciate special people in my life, and the cost of liberty. I learned to value the simplest moments."

Neither spoke as they entered the royal courtyard. Long red stone terraces led through magnificent 12th century arches and portals. Instantly they were swallowed into the crowd, lured inward by flowing acoustics of classical music from the pipe organ, with accompanying trumpets.

Rosa squeezed Adam's hand and shivered with anticipation as costumed minstrels circulated past to entice them to join in the jigs. In the spirit of the moment, she kicked up her toes for an instant with her hands on her hips, then blushed at Adam.

The shrill, melodic flute of the Pied Piper of Hamelin led a parade into the gardens, with a queue of children dressed as rats zigzagging behind in an orderly line.

"As a child, I learned from Robert Browning about the terrible tragedy, but history will have a far better memory than me," Rosa said.

"There are many legends. As I heard it, Johann Wolfgang told of the Pied Piper stealing all the children of Hamelin because the wicked mayor refused to pay for his services.

But whatever the true story, Heidelberg is free of rats," he joked.

"The flute music is so overwhelming that I could be tempted to follow too."

"So is it a flute I need to learn to play?" Adam quipped.

"Adam, I've been here for almost two weeks now. Every day I look forward to seeing you. You don't need a flute."

. . . To capture my heart.

Outside the castle, the drifting aroma from a vendor sparked Adam's appetite. He pointed to the foot of the incline.

"Braised bratwurst, Rosa—can I tempt you? Do you eat sauerkraut and mustard with yours?"

"Carts in New York sell sausage dogs, but I've actually never had one."

"Well, you'll never have one better than in Heidelberg. Herr Buchholtz is a second generation at this, and his are the finest."

"So how can I refuse?" she smiled. "But regular mustard. Not the hottest one! And a cold beer to wash it down . . ."

The bratwurst house had stand-up tables, and Rosa and Adam downed them quickly.

"I'm a bratwurst convert now. It was as you said."

She dabbed her lips with a paper napkin, but most of her lipstick came off with a smear of mustard. With a touch up, she turned her attention back to Adam.

"Before you leave, Rosa, I want you to see a special delicatessen near Abel's, one of my favorites. We'll send a hamper of German sausage and mustards to New York as a treat for Will and Edgar."

Rosa had noticed Adam's more frequent references to her boys, and his interest in them.

"That's a kind gesture, Adam. A wonderful idea."

The sky was magical, lit by the full moon and stars as Adam promised. With rental skates, they circled for most of an hour, gazing at each other as they danced to *A Christmas Waltz*.

"It's a beautiful night. Thank you—I'll never forget it." Her ankles ached, but she couldn't let go of this. Adam held her tight in the last dance, and never took his hand away from hers.

"I'm sorry if I crunched your hand," she said. "But I needed you to hold me up."

"I wanted my hand to be crunched," Adam kidded.

She stood up from the bench to take it all in—the castle and the bridge, the Christmas lights. Skating under the stars. Adam.

"You know I go back to New York on Tuesday?"

"I know, Rosa. But we're still here in this moment. Don't wish away time."

"You are a wise man and I am so lucky to have you, especially during all of this . . ."

"Perhaps in the summer, when the mountains are green, you could come back for another visit with your boys."

"The summer . . . these last ten days have been like a lifetime for me. I don't want to think about next summer."

Sitting again with her arm into the crook of Adam's elbow, she leaned her head. "Would you consider coming to New York sometime for a visit?"

"Are you ready for a big discussion, Rosa?"

She felt his body tense, and hadn't expected his reaction, nor was she able to respond, as the tone in his voice felt like a dart of pain in her heart.

An oompah band began the Schuhplattler German folk dance, and the crowd cheered as dancers twirled and kicked, slapping the soles of their shoes.

"I guess you've been saved by the band," Adam said. "Shall I take you home now, Rosa?"

That didn't come out right. I want to tell Rosa how much she means to me. Every day is more of a struggle. In my heart I know that I have fallen in love with my cousin's wife. That sounds like a crime.

He knew that things had been said that couldn't be taken back. He also knew he didn't want anything less.

I need to know that she has the same feelings too.

16

December 18, 1962, Repairing Bridges

Walking into the apartment, Rosa felt abandoned and lonely. Letting her body sag into the armchair, she began to sob. She had held back these tears and fears since the moment she laid eyes on Adam.

"It's not fair to mix them up. Jake was the love of my life, but he's gone. He would want me to go on with my life. Then there's Adam, my pillar, who reads my every feeling. Perhaps I'm not being fair to rely on him so much. He's a good man. He's given me no real reason to assume that he cares for me as I do him."

Her chest ached from the tears and exhaustion. She closed her eyes to recall the happier moments from the evening, and fell asleep for the night in the chair.

She opened her eyes as the morning bells of the Church of the Holy Spirit echoed across from the market square.

In the mirror, she was shocked at her tear-stained face. "Oh, dear Iris, where are you when I need heavy advice?"

Blubbering in self-pity, she decided a hot shower would be invigorating and get her stamina back to face the day.

"I promised to finish Abel's manifest and that's close. I'll drop in today on Mr. Bachmann like Adam asked. There's no point in crawling back into my little mouse house. Buck up, Rosa Stanford."

She packed a cart with clothing donations for the Providence Church and lugged it down the staircase. At 10:30 she heard Ludwig Bachmann sweeping in front of the store, and as she opened to leave, Ivan Atkinson, was in the hall with his workmen.

"Hello, Mrs. Stanford. I hope we haven't inconvenienced you with our work."

"Not at all, Ivan, but I should mention that I'll be leaving for New York on Monday. Adam will have Power of Attorney for the estate, so you can discuss any further issues with him."

"Perhaps the three of us could meet on Saturday. But I have a question now, if you don't mind, Mrs. Stanford."

"Of course, Ivan."

"My men hear tapping sounds and what I would describe as muffled music from somewhere below. Do you know what that would be?"

"Funny you mention that, Ivan. I've heard the same noises, but I don't have an answer. Perhaps Adam might have a suggestion. I don't have an arrangement to see him today."

The words stung as she said them.

Ludwig Bachmann greeted Rosa on the outer walk.

"Good morning, Rosa. God bless you, dear, for your generosity to me and my family. The clock shop is my dream come true. It's been my family's only craft for the last two hundred years. Please come in for a visit."

Grateful for the companionship, she obliged.

The ticking metronome and smooth rhythm of the clocks was soothing to her fragile soul. The clockmaker had a twinkle in his eye as if amused by her intrigue.

"This is kind of you, Herr Bachmann. I enjoy your company and I couldn't be more proud that the clock shop is possible for you. From this day forward, I'll forever have an affinity to clocks, no matter where I go."

Bringing a pair of stools from the work room, the clockmaker set a kettle on a hot plate for tea.

"Mr. Bachmann, if a customer comes in, you should attend to them and I'll wait for you here."

At that moment she heard the muffled music, and she studied the floor and walls, but to be polite she kept her curiosity to herself.

"Good," Bachmann answered. He didn't seem to notice her searching the walls. The room was large and crowded with supplies, gears, chronometers and pendulums waiting for their turn, and various boxes of clock-making parts.

"Would you tell me more about the Armbruster family? While here, I've been obliged to deal with widow stuff and I'm afraid I've neglected good friends. I want to be a better friend to Adam, not to simply accept his kind-heartedness every day."

"I know what you're saying and how you feel, Rosa. I am wise with years and I've seen my children and grandchildren through ups and downs in relationships. But you should always let it brew—like a cup of tea until it's exactly the way you like. Block out stresses of the day and focus on the person you are with—let them get to really know you. We naturally put up our guards even during every day events, and the other person doesn't always make the correct assumption."

"I'm glad I came here for our visit this morning, I miss my friends at home as they would also give me encouragement and advice, and I would feel supported."

"Dear child, you ask about the Armbrusters, but I see the truth. You are asking about Adam in particular."

Rosa's cheeks blushed.

"He has the eyes of my deceased husband, and I get confused. I don't know when I am being disloyal, and I need to be honest with myself and with Adam. I'm afraid that I do care more for him than I should."

The kettle was about to sing as the customer bell rang.

"I'll fix the tea, Mr. Bachmann. Your customers need you."

Dunking a teabag into each mug, she watched the discoloration seep into the boiling water. She didn't like hers strong and took hers out first. Mr. Bachmann seemed like a man wanting his tea stronger and she waited. At her last visit, she saw him take cream and sugar, and she prepared it to be ready.

Cradling the mug in her fingers, her eyes were drawn to the swirls, and she leaned in close.

I see the clouds I've let into my life here, and I have not been honest with the person that means the most to me.

Herr Bachmann returned and smiled as he observed.

"Have you found any answers there yet, my dear? Take your time and let your soul speak to your heart."

"You are indeed wise and I have learned a lesson. But I still need an answer to my question, Mr. Bachmann."

The clockmaker leaned back on his stool and straightened his back. Tucking his thumbs behind his suspender straps, he prepared to make his revelation to Rosa.

"Adam was very close to his grandfather, and spent more time upstairs than at his own home. He was always selfless and brave and took the loss of Abel badly. He became reclusive and Florentine thought he was despondent. I remember a time in the early 40's when Adam might have been 7 or 8 years old. He asked his father if he could enlist in the war to defend his country. He practiced marching and carried my broom like a rifle to guard our shop." Ludwig boomed with laughter at the vision.

"That was brave, as Hitler ruled Nazi Germany from 34 to 45, and he could have been shot for his insolence. Those boys, Jake and Adam, were born into a world of hatred and fear. Abel was proud of their strength in overcoming the losses from their youth. Even during the terror of Hitler, both boys had an admirable sense of duty, and had a sense of humor. But for a child . . .

"We all scattered for survival during the war, but afterwards Adam had changed. He was no longer happy and adventurous. He joined his father's barrister firm as a dutiful son should, and his parents were pleased when he married the daughter of one of Bogdan's associates. They were good on the outside, but I can't say it brought him happiness like you'd hope for in a marriage."

"I'm sorry for these stories," Rosa said. "I can't imagine growing up in a society like that. My family has been blessed to live in a democracy and take our freedom for granted. Adam said Astrid died soon after their marriage of cancer."

"Is that what he said? No, it was a car accident. It wasn't Adam's fault, but a truck collided with their car on the Heidelberg Road from Frankfurt. He never forgave himself. Adam carries a few scars, but Astrid lost her life. You have probably noticed that he doesn't drive often, instead he hires a car and chauffeur."

"We've been able to walk most everywhere we want to go."

"Rosa, dear child, it was clear to me the first day he brought you into my shop that you are not his client."

"But I am, Mr. Bachmann. It is not right that you suggest otherwise."

The clockmaker smiled warmly at her naivety, but he was endowed with rare patience and understanding, and was determined to speak to her heart. "Are you saying it's not right for you or Adam if he feels something other than a business relationship?"

"Then you know my dilemma?"

"Everything in life does not come at face value; it is full of secrets and it takes time to steep. Don't fear the distance of time yet to come, respect the distance of today."

Her voice quivered. "I have to go home to my boys, but I don't want to leave him. I'm afraid I have hurt his feelings, and perhaps he doesn't feel as you think, Mr. Bachmann."

"Don't worry child, love is a language of its own. When hearts are meant to be together, they find a way."

Rosa sighed with relief as she stepped off the stool. "You are a dear man, Mr. Bachmann, and you remind me a great deal of my grandfather. Perhaps you are more a match maker than a clockmaker," she teased.

"That is a compliment, I'm sure." The clockmaker chortled, and she rose on her toes to plant a kiss on the old man's cheek.

"I will know later today if Adam comes looking for me, as there's no business reason to see me today. Life is short and I'm planning to embrace Heidelberg today. Only a few days remain and I won't leave with any regrets."

"Did you know, Rosa, that the most romantic place in town is the Elizabeth Gate at the castle? You will see—he will come."

Strengthened with new life in her step, Rosa set out toward Old Town with the donation cart for the Providence Church. The joy in the air made her feel child-like, and she wanted to find the German dancers that performed folk dances by the Tree of Knowledge.

At the lederhosen kiosk she booked a dance lesson and tried her best to follow the lead dancers. She didn't acquire the skill, but laughed until her sides hurt, satisfied with her attempt.

Edgar and Will would look adorable in lederhosen. Perhaps before I leave.

From a patisserie at the Kornmarkt square she took a soup and homemade bread to a bench outside, and in contentment she drifted again to the previous evening. "If Mr. Bachmann is wrong, I am making a fool of myself."

A live nativity manger was setting up a few feet from her, with donkeys, sheep, and costumed participants enacting the birth of Jesus. Carols in German were piped out, with sporadic voices joining in song across the square. Rosa put aside her shy nature and gathered courage, first to hum with them, then to sing *Away in a Manger* and *We Three Kings* at her fullest voice as the play continued.

It is right that I have this time to myself. I was so focused on the estate I'd forgotten the meaning of Christmas. When I get home, my boys will be in our own play at St. Mary's and then it will truly be Christmas. Herr Bachmann was right, Christmas is in the heart.

At his office, Adam paced from the window to his desk and back. He refused to take business calls, and with every effort to start his work, his thoughts were on Rosa.

He phoned the Brand residence at noon, intending to ask her about the inventory, but there was no answer.

After lunch, he walked over and found Atkinson and the museum employees busy, but no Rosa.

"Ivan, have you seen Mrs. Stanford?"

"Not since I arrived this morning. She was on her way out."

"Do you know where?"

Ivan shook his head, and Adam ran down the stairs.

Today was Friday, and he was pressured to conclude the museum agreement and the Power of Attorney for the estate. At the square, he scanned every direction, then returned reluctantly to his office to await a transatlantic call. The afternoon didn't fare any better for him.

I hope she's alright. It's my fault. I've never felt such urgency before.

By 5 p.m. it was dark and his concern turned to worry when repeated calls remained unanswered. At a quickened stride, he went up the stairs and let himself in. The apartment was empty.

At the street, he practically bumped into Mr. Bachmann.

"Hello there, Adam."

"Have you seen her?" His voice had escalated to frantic.

"It's alright, Adam. I reminded her that she'd have the best view of Heidelberg from the Elizabeth Gates on the hill.

You know it's the highest and most romantic location in all of town. She's been waiting for you all afternoon."

"Did she talk with you, Mr. Bachmann?"

"She is heartbroken on this journey. Not once, but she thinks it is twice. When did you last see her? Perhaps you can pick up where you left off."

Adam started to pull away when Ludwig called him back. "You are both too worried about hurting the other."

He gave a farewell wink. "Trust your heart, Adam."

On the bench beside the grand arches overlooking Old Town, Rosa shivered with a cup of hot mulled wine. After her talk with the clockmaker, she'd been confident Adam would come.

The clock in the church steeple struck 6 p.m.

He's not coming!

Below on the terrace, a white carriage with a team of shiny black horses stopped at the entrance to the courtyard, and a lone occupant disembarked.

It was Adam, bounding up the stairs to Rosa, waiting on her bench at Elizabeth Gates.

17

December 19, Mission Accomplished,

Coming to a stop a few feet from Rosa, Adam watched the face of the woman he knew he loved, and he could no longer resist taking her in his arms. He knew he loved her in a way he hadn't known before.

"Rosa, I'm so sorry. I understand our situation is awkward and I didn't want to intrude on your grief. Since the day I met you, I've had this burning passion to hold you."

Rosa was on her toes, clinging to Adam. "I came to rely on you every day and today when you didn't come, I understood that my heart was broken. I've never wanted to see you more, then I feared you weren't coming. But fortunately, I have a Wise Man in the shop below."

"Yes, the Wise Man of Heidelberg. He said he was closing shop but I believe he was waiting for me, to make sure I came looking in the right place."

Adam caressed her face and gently kissed her forehead, her cheeks, and then her soft lips.

"Oh, Adam, what do we do? It pains me to have to leave you, but my boys need me back home."

"For starters, I've hired this romantic horse and carriage. I'd be honored if you would spend the evening with me, Rosa. I do believe Mr. Bachmann has orchestrated our destiny, whatever that may be. He is a strange man, Rosa, I have many curious stories to tell you."

The hames jingled at the high steps and swaying of the horses, as the driver steered the team into the snowy night.

It was after midnight when Adam kissed Rosa goodnight at the door beside the clock shop. She watched him disappear across the common toward Armbruster's; then preparing to go upstairs, she glanced sideways through the clock shop window, seeing a glimmer of light at the back.

On the staircase, she heard the familiar repetitive tapping and stopped to listen, switching off the hallway lamp. With her eyes accustomed to the darkness, she knelt on the stair riser, leaning her eye to a crack where a sliver of light beamed. She then put her ear close, and attuned to the slightest sound or movement, she heard bells jingling.

I've never given thought to what's on the first floor, but the building is much larger than the clock shop space. It barely takes a quarter of the floor in the blueprints. Something else is under the Brand apartment, something I've overlooked. I wonder if Adam knows about this. Surely, he would have mentioned it.

With eyes wide, she strained through the tiny aperture to see a jolly figure dressed in red.

Ah, it's like the cloak hanging in the shopkeeper's workroom on the day I met Mr. Bachmann. And there is the tapping and humming again—they're old German Christmas carols.

Rosa continued past the apartment, up to the third floor to look out the back from the rooftop terrace. Out on the parapet, she had the advantage of moonlight, but most of the town around Brand's had gone to bed, with very few lamps aglow.

Creeping toward the edge of the roofline, she heard a commotion below, and crouched beside the chimney to peer into the back lane. The open courtyard was dusted with fresh snow and a scattering of hay. Tucked in the corner of the yard, a large object was covered in a canvas tarp. From the edges, she could see that the object was on sleigh rudders.

No kidding . . . Santa's sleigh. I must be dreaming.

Focused on the dark scene below, her eyes adjusted to the light of a soft glow of yellow beams drifting from the back windows on the first floor. Then the creaking of barn doors. She froze, not to be seen. Below in the moonlight was a rotund red cloaked gentleman, leading an antlered deer toward a bale of hay.

When the jolly figure stood tall, he arched his back and tucked his thumbs behind Mr. Bachmann's suspenders.

That's him . . . that's Ludwig Bachmann! That's Santa!

The echo of a jolly Ho-Ho-Ho brought two child-like characters out to the yard. They were not unfamiliar when she thought back to the flow of odd customers coming and going from the clock shop. Both were in bright red and green Alpine lederhosen and chattered in a language she didn't understand.

Rosa held her breath as she watched the fantasy below, with the red-cloaked man, two workers and a reindeer. She silently let out her breath, and when one of the helpers glanced her way, she gasped. The noise immediately ceased and the gentleman shielded his hand on his forehead to look up at her with curiosity, then gave her a knowing wink.

Pulling back from the edge, Rosa's eyes felt heavy and sleepy. Struggling to keep them open was useless, but she felt the warmth of a gentle whisper in her ear.

"Rosa, I'll being seeing you in New York in a few days. Take this with you and I will bring your Christmas wish. Believe in me."

The morning sunshine filtered onto Rosa, curled up in Abel's chair. She blinked and opened wide, as if she'd been in a magical dream, wondering if the secret of downstairs were real. In her palm was a tiny snow globe, and she held it up to the light—a miniature courtyard and Santa Claus, as in her dream.

How can this be?

Today was Sunday, and she'd prepare for her trip, but at this moment she could think of nothing else but seeing Adam. Torn between leaving him and reuniting with her boys, she knew that decisions couldn't be put off any longer.

I owe it to Adam to tell him that he alone has my heart. I'm no longer confused. When I look in his eyes, I only see Adam and want no one else. Do I want to be noble with that adage of letting something go if you love it, and if it's meant to be it will return? No, I don't want that risk.

For Adam, Heidelberg was small and empty without Rosa, and she hadn't even gone. It was a critical crossroads in his life, choosing either the fire in his heart that he was compelled to follow, or the family loyalty and responsibility to the firm.

"It seems like an eternity since I left her at Abel's, and my heart aches. It isn't business anymore, it's my heart, my future."

From the parlor window, she saw his outline, grabbed a sweater and ran down the stairs to meet him in the courtyard. Folding herself into his embrace, she lingered until she thought she might cry with joy.

"Last night was a whirlwind, Adam, and I'm not sure if I told you how much I love you. I can't leave you with any doubts about that."

"I wish you didn't have to leave me at all. I can't go back to life here without you. Rosa, I'm afraid I see things in a different way. We should go to a patisserie and talk about this situation we've found ourselves in."

"Let me get my coat and boots. I'll be right back."

Rosa darted back upstairs leaving Adam outside the clock store. On Sunday mornings the shops were generally closed, so there was no sign of Mr. Bachmann and few pedestrians, other than stragglers on their way to church.

A gust of December wind caused Adam to look to the sky as it darkened with storm clouds. He raised his coat collar to his chin and shoved his hands into his pockets for warmth.

Something cold and round was deep in his left pocket. He had felt that shape before, but years before as a boy, when St. Nicholas gave him a similar object—a tiny snow globe with a miniature grandfather and small boy at the Christmas hearth. It was a treasure he never lost track of during the war, and was a reminder of his grandfather.

Over the years, his curiosity had risen many times about activities in the back workrooms of the clock shop, and as a boy, he imagined Ludwig Bachmann wearing the great red cloak, and accepted he was one of Santa's helpers.

He didn't have time to remove it from his pocket to inspect, as he heard Rosa coming on the stairs.

I know who put it here. My dear friend and matchmaker.

The Christmas Market was the busiest she'd seen, as the season's momentum and crowds had grown in the final week. "This is my last chance for souvenirs, and I'm packing one of Abel's old suitcases with the extras I've accumulated."

"Please let me buy lederhosen for the boys," Adam said, "the whole gamut with caps and knickers, so they can participate in their heritage. Hopefully they'll be able to come to Heidelberg soon and I'll meet them."

"I love your instincts about me and my family . . . and yes, I want very much for them to see Heidelberg too."

With purchases from the German wear hut, they settled at a patisserie, each sipping on coffee, waiting for the other to begin the long awaited conversation.

Rosa wiggled her hand under his as he rested his arm on the table. "Adam, I wish everything could be black and white."

He squeezed her hand. "Black and white? Is that cultural? I promise to study your expressions."

They both laughed, as she hoped he would understand. "It's a situation that can be clearly defined, you know, without complex answers." Her smile hid her unresolved pain.

Adam began. "My father is a quiet man and committed to his family and the community. Granddad Armbruster began the law firm long ago and took my father into the business right out of college. It was through a client that my father met my mother. She comes from an affluent family in upper class circles. Perhaps you see she thrives on being the center of attention and maintaining her social status.

"My father never really asked if I wanted to join the firm, he only assumed, and I didn't consider what other options I had. The same with David. I have been methodical in my work and understand law clearly, but I can't say it was my chosen profession."

"I'm not sure what you are saying, Adam. Are you happy being a lawyer?"

"Oh yes indeed, and I am considered to be a very good attorney. As you see, I specialize in estate cases and receive great pleasure from helping people resolve difficult situations."

"That bodes well then, because I see that we have a rather difficult one ahead of us. What do you suggest that we do?"

Rosa's eyes burrowed into his thoughts. "I want to give you the answer you deserve, Rosa. Can I ask for your patience until New Year's?"

"You've painted a realistic picture of your circumstances here, and of course I respect that."

His words echoed back to Rosa and although still unresolved, she was surprised at the relief she felt. She could now return to New York.

18

December 22nd, Adam has Horrific Flashback

Adam arrived with the chauffeured sedan at the break of dawn for the journey to Frankfurt. Everything that could be said had been spoken, and they clung to each other's hand. Both were deep in thought of what the future might hold, with the reality of responsibilities clouding the outcome. At the airport, Adam asked the car to wait.

He carried her luggage and never left her side through check in. At the gate, they kissed a final time and hugged tightly as tears streamed for Rosa. Once through, she looked back to see him watching, and with a wave, she disappeared out of sight.

Rosa boarded without event and chose a window seat. Looking out into the blue skies, the terrain of Germany and the Black Forest had disappeared, and she was transfixed in thought.

My future has turned upside down. Adam has changed my life forever.

Adam didn't immediately return to the sedan. Instead, he went directly back to the Lufthansa desk. He felt into his coat pocket and pulled out the tiny snow globe. Inside were a woman and two boys around a Christmas tree.

I know it was Ludwig.

Compelled to take control of his destiny, he took care of business matters at the desk, and returned to the hired car.

The return to town was typical as any other day until they came to a sharp turn. Heidelberg was visible around the corner, but a terrible sense of déjà vu overcame him.

This is the turn where Astrid died.

His forehead became heavy with sweat, with an attack of anxiety. On that fateful day there had been a slick of rain where a truck had dropped steel tubing on the highway. The car was propelled into a skid and he couldn't avert the slide into an oncoming semi-tractor trailer with a load of lumber.

In his head, he could hear the screams of his wife. It was an instant that would last an eternity. The windshield folded in, then swerving and squealing brakes until there was silence. Next he heard thuds and crunching, then sirens, but he couldn't find Astrid.

He remembered begging to know where his wife was. The medic leaned to offer him reassurance. "My partner is with her right now. I need you to work with me to get you out."

Ripping metal, the smell of diesel fuel, hot oil, steaming engines and a background of inaudible voices went on for a long time.

When Adam woke that day, he was in the Heidelberg Hospital with his parents at his bedside. His mother had been sobbing.

"What's happened? Where's Astrid?

His father moved closer. "Son, we're so sorry but Astrid didn't make it. She's in Heaven now!" Adam thought the words were incredulous.

The chauffeur repeated himself louder, the second time concerned with Adam's sudden behaviour in the back seat. "Mr. Armbruster, are you alright? Shall I pull over?"

"Oh, yes Guenther, I was recalling something unpleasant. No need to worry, but thanks for your concern."

"We'll be in Heidelberg momentarily."

19

December 22nd, Rosa arrives in New York

Hiring a taxi to Queens, Rosa's heart pounded with excitement and anticipation to see her boys. It had been almost three weeks, and at this moment nothing mattered but Edgar and Will.

From the street, she looked up and saw her boy's faces pressed to the cold glass of the bay window, watching for her. Leaving her luggage on the front stoop, she raced up the stairs as they squealed their delight.

Dropping to her knees at the door, she spread her arms and gathered them both in one swoop. Mrs. Fitch had stepped back to watch the joy of the reunion.

Will was jumping to kiss her cheek. "Oh, Mama, I missed you so much."

"I was thinking about you every day, what you'd be doing and wishing I were here with you."

Edgar seemed taller and much older. He quietly slid his hand into hers and urged her to come in so he could sit close while she told them everything.

"There's so much to tell you, I'm not sure where to begin. First of all, I know it's late here but let's postpone bedtime for a bit." She winked at Mrs. Fitch.

"Rosa dear, I'll come and have tea with you in the morning. Take your time with the boys and we can talk later."

The two snuggled onto the couch under her arms, and Edgar looked up with a serious face. "Mom, did you find Dad in Hildaberg?"

The words jabbed at her heart. Watching their hopeful eyes, she smiled wistfully and looked over at Jake's picture on the bureau by the door.

"You both understand the reason I went to Germany, don't you?"

"Yes, Mama. One of Dad's sisters died and you needed to tend to fairs," Will proclaimed.

Rubbing his curls, she held back her amusement.

"Dear Will, you are right in a way. It was Dad's ancestor who died and I had to attend to business affairs. It was his Grandpa Brand."

"Yes, Will," Edgar said. "Remember it was Dad's own German Grandpa. I told you about him while Mom was away." He was getting impatient for an answer to his question, and continued. "Mom, I explained to Will that Dad was either a POW or an MIA."

Rosa was startled at Edgar's knowledge. "Where did you hear that?"

"At school. Mrs. McPherson talked to us about wars and what happened to many of our American soldiers. Angus

Atkins' dad died on the battlefield and I've been sad for him. Many kids don't understand what it's like when the war is over and their father doesn't come home. That's the reason I get into a few bruisers now and then."

"I'm so sorry, Edgar." Rosa covered her mouth, then searched her son's face with her finger.

"When will they find Dad?" Will persisted.

"Your father had piloted a fighter jet near enemy space with two friends, and his plane was shot down. They got out using parachutes, but the enemy found them before they were rescued by Americans.

"Your Dad was wounded but got somewhat better in prison where he stayed for the three years we have been missing him. It's difficult to explain the fear of the people in Germany, those contained behind the Berlin Wall and denied freedom. Two months ago, your Dad decided he would try to help his friends escape to the free side of Germany.

"A few escaped, but I'm sorry. Your Dad was trying to help his friends and was shot."

There was a silent gasp in the room until Will burst into a tirade of tears. "Dad's not coming home, right?" Burrowing his head into Rosa's sleeve, he let go of his heartbreak.

Edgar, however, sat stoically, absorbing the information.

"Your Dad had cousins, aunts and uncles and many friends in Germany. While I was there, they got together and we had a funeral service in the same church where your Dad was baptized as a baby. It was a beautiful occasion with many kind words and talk of memories. Daddy died a hero so that we can live in a free country."

Rosa got up to collect the flag from her bags. Still folded in the presentation triangle, she placed it in Edgar's open hands.

"This is a tribute to Dad, an honor for an American soldier who gives his life during wartime." Then she laid out Jake's dog tags and his medal that Moretti gave to her, handing them to her sons to hold.

"Your father is buried in Heidelberg with his grandfather, but we should have a memorial service of our own here in New York. Our friends and relatives would want to come and share their stories and condolences. What do you think?"

"Yes, Mom, it will be like saying goodbye, right?" Edgar said, refusing to let his pain have the better of him, and feeling the shame of not having vivid memories.

The remaining days before Christmas were a whirlwind of business affairs and family arrangements. Rosa found it best to defer her return to the glove counter, and on Macy's insistence she agreed to a bereavement leave. The storybook displays in Manhattan were still the best places to take the boys, even the thrill of traveling by train and subway.

"Boys, we need our traditional trip to Macy's and Gimbel's. Who votes that we go today?"

Will tore off to the coat rack, pulling down his outer wear. "I'll get my gloshes, Mom." He managed to get the boots on himself, and she snickered at the sight, on the wrong feet. Enough snow had gathered for snowballs, and she waited for them to throw one or two at a tree before they were on their way. She was always patient, but especially today.

The fresh snowfall from the night before was already evaporating on the concrete sidewalks, with rivulets trickling into the drainage ditches.

In Manhattan, every light standard had a wreath that glowed in miniature white lights, each adorned with gigantic silver bells, and the storefronts were more beautiful than she remembered.

At Macy's, Elmer Harris jingled his bell and tousled Will's hat. As each boy dropped a coin in the kettle, he embellished his wishes with his jolliest laughs. "Thank you, and the merriest of Christmases to your family this year, Mrs. Stanford."

At the train window, they came to a full stop, watching elves taking carloads of gifts from the North Pole, with the flashing lights and whistles of the engine drawing their oohs and aahs.

"Toyland is on the upper floor, boys. Should we start with a visit to Santa?"

Will was on his toes in anticipation. "Yippee."

"Sure Mom," Edgar said. "I'll take Will and we'll get in the lineup."

"Stay together in this line. I'll pick something up and be right back. See the big clock on the wall over there?"

"Mom, won't you watch me on Santa's lap?" Will asked.

"Of course, dear. I'll be right here watching."

Collecting her layaway gifts at the next counter, she was back in their sight in minutes. At last it was Will's turn, and Rosa drew close to hear the conversation.

"Merry Christmas, little boy," Santa said. "What's your name?"

"William Stanford, Sir, and I want a Dad for Christmas."

"Ho, ho, ho, that's a tall order young man. Do you have someone in mind?"

"I was thinking since my Dad died in war that we could get a new one." Her eyes glassed up at Will's innocent gaze into the jolly man's face.

Santa Claus glanced at Rosa and winked.

Her face hid the pain she felt, as her children expressed such a poignant loss and need in their lives.

"I'll do my best, William Stanford, but sometimes these things don't come exactly on Christmas Day. It might take a little extra time."

"I know but I thought I'd try."

"Don't you want new toys?"

"No, just the Dad."

Will climbed off Santa's lap and returned to Rosa with a stern face and a tear in his eye.

Edgar was next, and whispered something incoherent into Santa's ear.

"Edgar Stanford, you must be William's big brother. I must say you boys are not selfish at all, and I'll put an extra team at the workshop on your request—you are a special family."

Santa, touched by the boys' emotional pleas, raised his hand to halt the line and took a moment's break with a hankie and a glass of water.

Rosa gave them each a five dollar bill and they dallied in Toyland buying presents for each other before they'd move to Gimbel's down the street. Shelves brimmed with boxed toys, spinning tops, puzzles and board games to hold any child's imagination.

After the day on their feet, Rosa knew the boys would be tired and hungry, and just as Will was about to become cranky, she knew to intercept.

"Let's get back to Macy's dining room, boys. I can't wait to eat!"

It was a typical diner layout, and best of all were its plush, soft cushioned chairs. She thought about removing her boots to free her aching feet, and remembered the lieutenant warning her of the consequences of swelling.

Rosa picked the signature chicken pot pie with salad and the boys toiled over whether to put cheese on their burgers.

"Two cheeseburgers for the boys, and chocolate milk."

Last stop was the grand old confectionary, with polished mahogany counters taller than Will, and colorful glass jars filled with lollipops, licorice, peppermint twists and almost any imaginable temptation. Rosa found a rich, dark fruit cake and collected a sack full of candy canes and ribbon sweets for Christmas Day.

On the Queensboro train, Will fell asleep first, then Edgar.

Jake's memorial service was set for December 27th. Edgar and Will were assigned to prepare letters in their neatest printing for their Uncle Lloyd to read, each with a favorite memory of their father. Edgar would help Will, and they got at it right away together.

Edgar asked if they could then sort family photos for a scrapbook, and Rosa knew that keeping busy was therapeutic. Will had stopped crying, but Edgar hadn't yet shed a tear to allow the grief.

The house seemed different to Rosa, as she started organizing her life with definition and determination. At night, she realized she no longer needed to cradle Jake's pillow for comfort, and on the first nights home the two boys crept into her room and snuggled until asleep.

———————

Adam was at the office early the morning after Rosa left. It was six-thirty and still dark on the streets when Bogdan Armbruster arrived at his office. He was startled to find a desk lamp burning in Adam's office.

"Good morning, son. I'm surprised you're here so early. You need time off on the holidays. I know the Brand estate has been a lot on your plate, and you must be tired and stressed."

"Thanks, Dad . . . but we need to talk."

Bogdan knew something was troubling his son, and he closed his door. His words were kind and gentle. "I'm listening, Adam. We don't often have father and son chats, and we are long overdue."

Adam cleared his throat and searched for the right words. The last thing he wanted was to disappoint his father.

"Have I changed since Rosa was here?"

His father smiled. "Yes, I've watched that. You are a lot like me, Adam—we are deep and thoughtful, whereas David is more gregarious and simplistic like your mother. Each is a quality to be certain, but you and I need our hearts to rule our heads."

Adam sighed his relief at his father's insight and nodded his acknowledgement.

"I've been tortured since Rosa arrived and I'm afraid there is no return for me. I never before gave credence to love at first sight, but from the moment I saw her at the airport, my heart fluttered with fear."

"Love is not to be feared, Adam, it should be embraced." Bogdan walked to the window and stared into the darkness, and returned with the courage to speak what needed to be said.

"If I may regress to my own circumstances at your age, I would have to confess that I fell madly in love with one of my peers at the University. She was not German, nor from a family of standing. I allowed my parents' opinions to guide my decisions."

"I'm sorry, Dad."

Bogdan snapped back from his pained memory. "This is no reflection on your mother, of course. She is a wonderful woman, wife and mother, but I admit only to you that I regret losing my first love. When times are tough, I wonder what might have been. But then alas, I am gratified with my choice and have two fine sons that mean the world to me."

"Thanks for making this easier for me."

"Oh no, Adam, don't think for a second this will be easy, but I understand and support whatever decision you make. What are you going to do about that passion in your eyes when you mention her name?"

"I have made up my mind—I'll go to her in New York. There's a small business matter in arrangements for the trust fund, but I cannot bear my days here without her. When I'm there, I'll look for a position. If I can't obtain a green card, I'll have no choice but to return to Heidelberg. If it comes to that, hopefully Rosa and her boys will come with me."

Bogdan smiled. "Now who's going to tell your mother?" The pair shared a hearty laugh, with the tension relieved.

At 9 a.m., he met with Ivan Atkinson, then stopped at the travel office to arrange a hotel close to Rosa's Queens apartment. At home, he broke the news to his mother and David, and they both said the right words of support that he had hoped to hear.

He cleaned up an old leather case from the attic and wrapped the parcel from the clock shop. Beside it was pair of his treasured childhood train engines, his grandfather's old St. Nicholas boots and a Father Christmas cloak that had been in the Armbruster family for many generations. Last was a folding wooden walking stick.

My schedule will be tight but I have a good map to get around. I'll be too late to make the St. Mary's pageant but Rosa and the boys should be home by 9:30.

He looked through the curtains to a full moon. Somewhere beyond, he was sharing the same moon with Rosa, and he repeated the words in his head of the nostalgic wartime song by Billy Holiday, *I'll be Seeing You.*

20

December 24, Christmas Eve

*R*osa woke to find Edgar at her door with a bundle of burlap potato sacks, tea towels and a length of rope. It was Christmas Eve, and he raised a surprise that she'd forgotten.

"Mom, what about my shepherd's costume for tonight?"

Will was too young for a pageant speaking part and would be more content in the pew with his Mom.

"But I want a costume too," Will said. "What can I wear?"

The thought of lederhosen struck her like a bolt of lightning.

"As a matter of fact, I have the perfect outfit for you. In Heidelberg, I spent a lot of time with your Dad's cousin, Adam Armbruster. He was very good to me and asked about you boys many times. He insisted on sending home a gift for you."

"A present? Can I open it?"

"Sit here on the sofa and I'll bring them out."

Ripping the tissue, Will shrieked. "It's marvellous, Mom. But what is it?"

"See—these are britches, suspenders, knee socks, a shirt and even a hat. It's a traditional German outfit that all the boys in Heidelberg wear on special occasions."

"Can I wear mine to the pageant, Mom?" Will pleaded.

"I don't see any reason you can't."

Edgar remained on the couch, letting his fingers run over the colorful embroidery, but his thoughts were miles away.

The church was packed for the concert, however Vivian saved room for Rosa and Will. Edgar joined his cast back stage, and he was a standout shepherd minding his flock as the choir sang *While Shepherds Watch Their Flocks* and *Hark the Herald Angels Sing*.

The pageant proceeded without calamity, but Rosa's mind drifted to Adam continuously.

I wish he were here.

———————

On the morning of Christmas Eve in Heidelberg, Adam was dressed for the flight before the sun rose. Bogdan insisted that Florentine say her farewell at the house, and he drove Adam to the train terminal for the shuttle to Frankfurt.

It was dark again by the time the jetliner touched down at LaGuardia. A redcap porter collected his suitcases and Adam waited in the taxi queue, checking his watch. From the cab, he observed the buildings of the Manhattan skyline. It was as peaceful as Christmas Eve should be, with the New York sky bringing a quiet, gentle snowfall to hush the city.

It would be too much of a walk from the hotel to the brownstone, and the driver waited as he dropped his bags.

Minutes later he came out of the hotel wearing tall black boots, Father Christmas's cape, with the walking stick and a red sack of gifts.

The driver leaped from the car, beaming at the sight. "Best Christmas ever," he gushed en route to the brownstone.

While Adam stood on the sidewalk outside, Rosa, Will and Edgar were setting out Santa's snacks and carrots for the reindeer. The stockings were hung on a false hearth that was lit with a glow lamp, and Santa letters were pinned to the stockings.

"Mom, are you going to read *'Twas the Night Before Christmas* like Dad always did," Edgar asked.

"I don't remember that, Edgar," Will scowled.

"You were too little."

Rosa's head turned sharply at a sound outside. A soft carol was playing on the Marconi, and she turned down the sound, listening with her finger to her lips to quieten the boys.

"What's that?" she said with a lilt in her voice. She pointed toward the roof, thinking she'd take advantage of the noise. "Maybe reindeer hooves."

"It's not on the roof, Mom. It sounds like heavy boots on the stairs." Edgar yielded to the fantasy, with his eyes wide with curiosity.

"Maybe carolers then to sing to us. Shall we see?"

Rosa opened the door in gest and froze. Before her was a tall man with a white beard and long hair, and a Father

Christmas cloak like she only imagined in storybooks. But the green eyes revealed the ruse to her.

"Why Edgar and Will, this is Father Christmas. I believe he has followed me from Germany." Overwhelmed, she cupped her hand over her mouth.

"Ho, Ho, Ho, and Merry Christmas. Is this the Stanford house?"

"Yes, yes, it is." Will was beside himself jumping up and down, still dressed in his lederhosen.

"May I come in? I happen to have three names here that are on my Nice list—Edgar, Will and Rosa. Would I be at the right house?"

Edgar watched his mother's face, trying to decide fact from fiction, but he saw she was absorbed with glee and surprise, and knew this had to be more than fantasy.

"Father Christmas, did you bring us presents?" Edgar urged, gesturing to the red sack at the door.

"You must be Edgar. I remember when your Dad was a boy, he looked just like you."

"You remember . . . my Dad?" Edgar was letting go of the possibility this man pretending to be Father Christmas could be fake.

"Indeed, I do. Every year he was on my Nice list. When he was a boy about your age back in Heidelberg, he asked me for a Sante Fe HO diesel train engine. It was cream and blue like this one."

From the sack, Santa pulled out the vintage engine, in pristine condition with headlights and a whistle.

Edgar's mouth was open and his eyes wide as he leaned to receive the treasure.

"And me, too?" Will said, right at Santa's knee trying to peer into the bag.

Rosa moved over behind Adam and rested her hand on his shoulder. Glancing up at her, Santa winked.

"For Will, I have a Lionel HO locomotive that puffs steam. I believe that one is red and black."

"Ooh." Will's fingers ran over the train and climbed up onto Adam's lap, hugging it.

Edgar tried one more test. "Father Christmas, did you forget to bring something for my Mom. She had a hard year and just came back from a funeral."

"Yes, your Mom has indeed been very good." Reaching into the bag, Adam pulled out a box wrapped in newsprint with a red bow."

Rosa sat in the arm chair, holding her breath as she untied the ribbon. As the paper fell away, she gasped, speechless at the magnificent Hansel and Gretel cuckoo clock. Setting it carefully on the floor, she went to Father Christmas and kissed him on the cheek, taking his available knee.

"Santa, how did you know this was the clock I wanted in Heidelberg?"

"I take great care to please all the special people on my list. The clockmaker there is a very intuitive man."

From the pocket folds of the cloak, he held out a miniature snow globe with a woman and two boys at Christmas.

"This magically appeared in my coat, but by then I had already made up my mind to follow you here.

Rosa went to a drawer in the hallway and returned with another miniature snow globe. "I believe the clockmaker gave this to me. You won't believe how it came into my possession, Santa. It was a preposterous fantasy, and I was convinced it was a dream. I hadn't told anyone, for feeling foolish."

Edgar moved next to Santa's foot, and settled with his legs crossed. "Did you know that my Dad died in the war?"

"Yes, a letter came to my shop in Heidelberg, where there's a kindly clockmaker who helps with the Santa mail. The Air Force sent us a list of good men who gave their lives so that you will never need to go to war. The clockmaker spoke with me in Germany and told be of the sacrifice of Captain Jacob Stanford. You must be very proud of him."

Will's tired eyes were wistful. "Mister, I'm proud of my Dad, but I'm sad I really don't remember him too good. He went away in uniform when I was still a baby. Would you come to our remembering service for my Dad? It'll be after Christmas."

"Why thank you, Will. I'm afraid I need to go back to the North Pole, but I could send your Dad's friend, Adam. If that's alright with you, of course. Adam knew your Dad like they were brothers."

"Like I know Edgar?"

"Yes, Will . . . like that."

Rosa's lip was trembling at their sweetness and endearing conversation, and adoringly watched the pair.

"Well lads, it's getting late," Santa said, and stood tall gathering up his empty sack. "You should be off to bed and I must get to the other children. There's much to do tonight. Merry Christmas boys."

"But . . ." Will called him back. "Can you read us '*Twas the Night Before Christmas*?"

"I'd be honored."

Will and Edgar tucked in at his sides on the couch, listening to every magical word. Before he finished, Will nodded off.

"Edgar, please stay here with Will. I'm going to see Father Christmas off at the door."

"Adam, I love you so much. You did something truly marvelous there for my boys. You're a wonderful man and I'm so happy to see you. Tomorrow is Christmas and you must come to my cousin Vivian's for the family dinner. She wouldn't hear of you not coming. I'll be there at three.

"I can hardly believe you are here with me in New York."

21

December 25, Christmas Day in Washington Heights

W ill and Edgar pounced on Rosa's bed at the first light of dawn on Christmas morning, begging to empty their stockings.

"Wash up first and brush your teeth." She rubbed the slumber from her eyes, as if it had been a dream. "I'm getting up, I'm getting up," she said.

Racing each other to the living room, the boys skidded to a halt at the tree. "Ooh look, Will, it *was* Santa. See, we don't have that kind of wrapping paper here."

Tearing the paper from Rosa's layaway presents, they wiggled and gibbered with delight at the parts for the train set.

"Don't forget the gift from Aunt Vivian and Uncle Lloyd. And you need to thank them today."

Will scrunched the wrapping as it tore.

"It's 'popoly, Mom."

Edgar burrowed far under the tree for a parcel he hid at the back. "This is for you, Mom. I used my whole five dollars on you . . . Will said it was okay."

"That is such a generous thing, Edgar. And thank you for your part in it too, Will."

The gift had two parts—a linen handkerchief with violets embroidered in the corners and a miniature bottle of rose cologne.

"It's wonderful, Edgar. They are two of the things I was really hoping for."

He sat back to digest his satisfaction. "Did you see that it came with your name on it?" He pointed to the word 'rose' that was changed by pencil to Rosa.

"That is too special!" Rosa gave Edgar a loving squeeze. "How did you spend your money, Will?"

"Here Edgar, open it." He shoved a collection of tape with bits of paper into his brother's face.

"Great scot!" Edgar said. "This is the best cat's eye I've ever seen." He poured out a bag of marbles that bounced across the floor including a marvellous blue and yellow one. "We can shoot marbles together, Will."

Gathering the strewn paper and folding the best of it, Rosa went to the kitchen to start breakfast.

"Are you men hungry?"

"No, Mom. We just want to play."

Rosa started preparation for a glazed apple turnip casserole and wondered what Adam was doing for Christmas morning.

The Watson house was across town in Washington Heights, near Sugar Hill in northern Manhattan. It was a

Victorian walk-up with a pretentious front walk, and an ornate gate that stood out from its neighbors.

The lace living room curtains were pulled back on sashes, centering an enormous, glittering blue spruce with flickering water candles that gurgled in brilliant colours, and draped with an avalanche of tinsel and angel hair.

Lloyd Watson was brushing the last traces of snow from the front threshold, and stepped out to meet Rosa's yellow cab. In his early forties, he had a round jovial face, and she'd often thought before that he'd have been a good Santa Claus in spite of his shorter than average stature.

"Hi, Uncle Lloyd," the boys echoed as they passed him in search of their Watson cousins.

Lloyd carried her casseroles and a Macy's shopping bag of odd-shaped parcels.

"Thank you, Lloyd, you are a godsend." She paused on the sidewalk to look at his face, searching for that 'knowing look' she needed for reassurance. "Did Vivian tell you about Adam?"

"If I'm not supposed to know, then no, but if you want me to know, then yes. You know, Rosa, I can always be trusted with your secrets."

"Of course, I know that, Lloyd. I'd be grateful if you'd take him under your wing. He just arrived last night and surprised the boys as Father Christmas. His costume was authentic and of course the boys don't know. I need to ease Adam into our family today and give him a chance to bond with Edgar and Will."

"Rosa, darlin', we're all looking out for you. Viv says that this might be the one. From the look in your eyes, I'll have to agree before even meeting the fella."

From the door she heard another cab, and rushed to the curb, and her heart fluttered at his sight.

He embraced and kissed her outside the taxi, then leaned inside for several shopping bags and a poinsettia. In his free hand he carried a boxed corsage.

Rosa turned around to discover Lloyd standing very close behind, and he stepped back. "Hello thar Adam, I'm Lloyd Watson, Rosa's brother-in-law. I'm pleased to meet you—let me help with your load."

"It's all my pleasure, Lloyd." But his eyes were on Rosa.

Vivian heard the strange voice from outside and stepped out behind Lloyd.

"Hallo, Adam." She waved her apron in the air and turned to Rosa. "Bring Adam in before he catches pneumonia." It was Vivian's way of saying she'd like a closer look.

Rosa gripped Adam's elbow and squeezed him, and rising to her tiptoes, she whispered, "I love you."

Inside was a melee of relatives: Rosa's Aunt Lil; her mother's sister and Uncle Sam; Isabel Murphy, a recently widowed soprano from the St. Mary's choir; and Charlie Wagner, an aged neighbor. A conglomeration of children circled on a race through the house, and Adam caught a glimpse of Edgar and Will on the fly.

Most of the women gravitated to the kitchen for meal preparations, but Rosa was reluctant to leave Adam's side.

"Come with me, Adam," Lloyd said. "I could use your muscle to help me haul up a folding table from the basement for the kids." Lloyd's charm and spew of small talk was not wasted on Adam.

"Right behind you, Sarge!" Adam teased.

All of Vivian's bests were already laid on the table, her new Christmas linen, her Sunday china, polished silverware, and crystal glasses. Beyond the dining room was the kid's table with paper hats and festive horns.

Suddenly, Will noticed the new stranger in their midst.

"Hi, are you my Dad's cousin from Garminy?"

"I am indeed, and you must be Will. Your Mom and Dad told me about you and I'm glad I'm meeting you. Please call me Adam."

Edgar was more curious, and edged closer. "You knew my Dad pretty good, right?" He was tentative in his handshake with Adam.

"I did, Edgar. I have plenty of stories to tell you."

As the turkey platter passed around the table, Rosa explained to Adam that it was the bird of feast, and there wouldn't be any carp. Every plate was heaped high from bowls of stuffing, mashed potatoes, yams, Rosa's turnip casserole, buttered carrots, sweet peas, braised cabbage, and sides of cranberry sauce and tureens of gravy.

Everyone wore crepe hats from the table crackers, and laughed and reveled at toasts of sparkling wine.

After dinner, Will gravitated to Adam.

"The big kids won't let me play, they think I'm too little. Maybe I can sit here and watch you play dominoes with Uncle Lloyd and Uncle Sam."

"Fine by me." Will took that as an invitation and climbed onto Adam's lap, with his arms on the table.

Edgar ran off again with his cousins, but made a point of inspecting Adam whenever he was near the living room.

Every Christmas, Sam and Lil hosted a guessing game with a secret code for only the pointer and a prearranged guesser. On another table, two men played an old fashioned crokinole game, and at the kitchen, Monopoly was spread on the table, with kids scrapping over who would be the shoe and the hat.

Will hardly left Adam's lap and was soon leaning against his chest, his eyes blinking heavily and ready to sleep.

"Vivian, unfortunately it's time for us to go home. May I use your phone for a cab?" Vivian and the woman from the choir went to the door to say goodnight, and they both hugged Rosa and then Adam to his surprise.

She sat close to him in the taxi. "Adam, I could use a hand getting a sleeping boy up the stairs. It's still early."

Adam lowered Will to his pillow without waking him and Rosa watched as he kissed Will's forehead.

Edgar was still in the living room, waiting with an open box of his Dad's dominoes. "Mr. Armbruster, I know how to play this. Will you play it with me before you leave? I used to do it with my Dad when I was little."

Adam squatted to the floor. "Edgar, it would be my honor to challenge any son of Jake Stanford to a game of dominoes. Tell me, did you always beat your Dad?"

"Not always, but sometimes. It didn't matter who won; I just liked playing games with him." Edgar was at last relaxed.

"Maybe you could tell me stories about Dad while we're playing."

Edgar glanced at Rosa for approval, and with a wink, she conveyed her pleasure that his guard was lowered. She loved his normal cautious instinct—that even at his tender age would have been to protect her.

"Since it is 10 o'clock and we've all had a full day, would you mind if Adam comes back tomorrow? But, of course, you have time for at least a story," Rosa suggested.

"Gosh, would ya, Mr. Armbruster?"

"Sure will. But Edgar, you can call me Adam if you like."

"Tomorrow Adam, you could help me with the new train engine I got from St. Nicholas."

"I love trains, too. It was one of my favorite things to do with your Dad, especially at Christmas at your age in Heidelberg."

Rosa watched from the arch between the kitchen and living room. Her arms were casually folded, and her head tilted to the side, unable to take her eyes off this wonderful man who had entered her life.

22

*T*his time at the parlour window, Rosa was joined with two small faces, eagerly squeezing to be the first to see the taxi pull up.

Will shouted first. "He's here, Mom. Adam's here!" He was wiggling on his knees onto the radiator, with his feet dangling with mismatched socks.

"I'll go out and help Adam find our apartment in case he forgot," Edgar blurted, and before a reply he was gone.

"Wait for me, I wanna come too."

Rosa stopped Will by the back of his shirt as he slid past.

"Hold on, Mister, you're in your stocking feet." She snickered seeing them. "And look at them. You know you're not allowed on the stairs without shoes."

"Aw gee, Mom." Will wormed himself free and bounded to the doorway as Adam and Edgar returned.

"I'm glad you came back."

Rosa snuggled into Adam's arm, but wanted appearances to be casual so the boys wouldn't see the burning romance.

From the door, his eyes lit up. He pointed to the coffee table. "Look boys! A box of track."

The Antik Toys box that Rosa brought from Heidelberg was open, and the two Christmas trains were on the floor.

"Adam, if you move the coffee table to sit around, I'll find the old box of cars."

Adam always dreamed of having a son of his own, and of days like this. "We've got this, Rosa."

She didn't hear, as she was already up the attic ladder to retrieve Jake's old boxes from his childhood collection. They'd been in the rafters since the first year of Jake's duty in Germany and not touched since.

Oh Jake, I wish you could see how wonderful things are with Adam here. I can see why you were both tight like brothers.

She pressed her hand to her heart with endearment. It seemed wrong for her to be so happy, when today, of all days, they'd be making arrangements for Jake's memorial service.

As the ladder sprang back up into the hall ceiling, Rosa saw three pairs of wide eyes watching for her, to see what she'd found.

Adam searched the dusty cardboard box for power switches, as Will squished close to him pulling out trees and a shanty hut and landscape materials. Edgar was rolling his new engine back and forth, testing it on the new track.

Rosa left them alone, but remained in demand. "Mom!" Come now," Will shouted, on all fours on the floor. "Come and see my locomoshun. Adam made the lights work."

She tied her apron strings around her back and moved close to inspect Will's new discovery. He rested on his elbows and waited for her reaction, finally looking at her. Then Adam and Edgar looked up too.

Her face glowed as she took it all in. "My goodness, the circle of track is so realistic with the bridges. And the St. Nicolas trains connect perfectly with the Macy's cars."

"We're about to connect the track circuit switch, Mom. We're going to call the station Stanford Depot—Dad would like that, wouldn't he?" Edgar said.

"He sure would. Now that you mention Dad, we have to prepare more for the special service tomorrow. Did you boys get the scrapbook finished?"

Neither of the heads raised to answer, "Uh ha . . . just about." She looked at Adam with a plea for help, but saw only a sheepish grin of how much he was enjoying the moment.

A new idea struck Will.

"Mom, can I wear my ladyhosen tomorrow—the one Adam sent me from Garminy?"

Adam answered first, sensing Rosa's exasperation in getting the boys' attention.

"Will, as handsome as you'll look in your new outfit, your Sunday suit will be more appropriate. I'm going to wear mine. How about it? And we can sit together like a family."

The words were barely out when he regretted sounding presumptuous, projecting himself into this new family without talking to Rosa about how it should be dealt with.

Edgar continued without concern. "Mom always has trouble with my tie on Sunday, Adam. Will you fix one of Dad's for me? His favorite was the blue and red stripes. He said it was patriotic."

"We'll do it together; and it certainly sounds patriotic."

Will's eyes pleaded, "I'm not big enough for a real tie. Mom makes me wear a bow tie with an elastic around my neck. It's dark blue. Will that be patioptic too?"

"I love your bow tie," Rosa said, "but if you want to wear one of Dad's, I'm sure Adam will help you fix it."

As Rosa called Lloyd and others about the service, Adam rounded up Edgar and Will, ready to glue into the scrapbook. He saw almost no pictures of Jake's childhood, and sorted through for the early ones with the boys. There were none together since they were very young.

Adam mulled over their reality, sensitive that the boys would have insatiable curiosity with their questions as they lived with scant memories of their father.

Leaning over the scrapbook, Adam told story after story of Jake's childhood adventures, and with wide eyes, they envisioned the pact of the brotherhood Adam had with their father. Whenever he stopped, they egged him for more.

"Tell us about the carp again?" Will asked.

Rosa heard it and put down her papers.

"You boys understand now about Adam being your Dad's cousin, but did he tell you that his very own mother was your Grandma Stanford's sister.

Will's hand waved in the air. "Then why is your name Armbruster?"

Rosa tried the comparison of herself to Aunt Vivian, being her cousin, and how their names changed at marriage.

It only confused Will further, and with a sigh, she resigned herself to change the subject.

"It's lunch time. Who's hungry?"

Adam rose from the table. "Let me make sandwiches, Rosa, and you continue with the ceremony details."

Both boys followed him to peer into the refrigerator.

"How about ham and cheese?"

"Yay . . . and can I get a pickle too? We have Garmin pickles that we call 'dill'."

"I'm with you, Will," Adam said.

At a knock at the apartment door, Edgar sprang from the table. "I'll get it. It might be important."

He opened it a few inches to peek out. A man in a brown US Postal uniform was panting from his run up the stairs with two large parcels from Heidelberg.

Adam was closest and signed for the packages and made room on the table. Will was the first to start picking at the brown wrapping paper.

"I believe, Rosa, this is the mantle clock for Mrs. Fitch . . . and the other, oh yes, the sausage and cheese hamper."

"My goodness, we've been so busy, I forgot about dear Mrs. Fitch. Will, would you mind knocking on her door and see if she'll come for tea, and we'll give her the present. I hope she likes clocks."

Minutes later, Will returned leading the regal Mrs. Fitch by the hand. Her eyes immediately took a critical view of the stranger in their midst.

"Excuse me, Mrs. Fitch. I heard much about you from Rosa when she was in Heidelberg. I'm Adam Armbruster, Jake's first cousin. I've come for his memorial service and to help out with the family."

"I see."

She wasn't easily swept off her feet with charm, but nonetheless offered her hand in greeting while maintaining a protective assessment.

"Mildred, we can't thank you enough for looking after Will and Edgar. You're a godsend and we love you. While in Heidelberg, I became acquainted with a marvellous old gentleman who is a clockmaker, an old world craftsman.

"I was smitten with this mantel clock and I had to have it for you for all your kindness. I'd like you to accept this." An after-thought struck Rosa, for the key in her handbag from Mr. Bachmann.

By nature, Mrs. Fitch was always in control of situations, and was momentarily flabbergasted. She lifted the clock with both hands and her eyes watered.

"It is indeed wonderful, Rosa, but this wasn't necessary."

"It's what I wanted to do. Now, would you like to join us at the church tomorrow? It's a small memorial gathering of Jake's old friends and relatives to celebrate his life."

The kettle whistled behind and Adam put his hand on Rosa's shoulder to stay. "I'll assemble the tea things."

From the kitchen, he watched as the women hugged and wiped away tears.

23

December 27, St. Mary's Memorial

*A*dam spent most of the morning organizing the boys. Their shoes were shinier than they'd ever seen, and standing them side by side, he dabbed their hair with a touch of Brylcreem, getting giggles from both.

In their breast pockets, he tucked crisp white hankies, then the three laid out ties sorted by color and began the elimination, one by one. With appropriate ties knotted, Will and Edgar tucked the long ends into their trousers.

Adam insisted on snapshots with Rosa's brownie camera. "This will be a day you'll want to remember." As they posed, Adam stopped. "Hey Edgar, where's your front tooth?"

"In my pocket," he grinned sheepishly. "I didn't want to make a big deal of it today."

"I'd like to hear about it later." Rosa said.

At St. Mary's Church, many folks arrived early, and all but Mrs. Fitch and the Watsons were strangers to Adam.

For the first time since arriving in New York, he dealt again with the perplexity of his new role in Rosa's life, as if he were watching from the outside.

At times, I feel like an imposter stepping into Jake's life and filling in as father to Will and Edgar. And yet I love her and long to hold her.

The boys got Rosa's final inspection before taking seats, and to Adam's surprise, Will reached for his hand.

Needing Adam's reassurance, Will looked up with trusting blue eyes like his mother's. "Come on . . . we can be sad together, right?"

Rosa took Adam's elbow, and with Edgar on her other side, the family was ushered to a pew beside the Watsons.

Curious eyes drew quick judgements about Rosa and this new man at her side. She bolstered her strength, knowing she was becoming the talk of churchy gossip, as pairs of older ladies adorned in hats were in whispers, pointing their heads her way.

I confess before God that Jake was the love of my life every day he was alive. I never gave another man a second thought. But now I know he'll understand that my heart seeks Adam. We've been so busy, I haven't asked if he's here to stay now. I'm afraid to ask.

Organ music filled the sanctuary with a crescendo of Jake's favorite hymn *Amazing Grace* by a small choir lined up behind the minister's platform.

Lloyd Watson spoke first on behalf of the family, then called on Jake's cousin Adam Armbruster.

He talked of his time with Jake as a child, then a beautiful reflection on his wife and family in recent days, remarking that Jake would be proud of Rosa, Will and Edgar.

Rosa remained stoic until the finale, when Isabel Murphy and her sister sang a patriotic duet of Eidelweiss from the Sound of Music, bringing many to tears.

Every word lingered and burned in Adam's heart, but he wasn't thinking of Jake at all.

The taxi ride to Queens was quiet except for Will talking about anything and everything, to monopolize Adam's attention. Rosa was reminiscing—it was the drive to the Heidelberg airport with Adam, both of them silent and looking out into a world of secrets and unknowns.

"Can we eat, everybody?" Edgar asked.

"I saw the perfect spot the other day on Maspeth—the Clinton Diner. Who's up for a family supper?" Adam said.

Rosa thought she'd melt with desire. She tilted her head to watch his face, then connected with his green eyes. She had closed one chapter and wanted to find out what lay in the future with Adam.

The diner was a display of red vinyl and chrome, and Rosa suggested a booth mid-section. She slid to the inside on the wide bench and nodded to Adam, patting the spot beside her. She hoped to sit close but stay inconspicuous, as she remained deliberate in concealing her attachment to Adam in the boys' presence.

Edgar took the empty bench across, however Will didn't. Instead, he climbed in tight beside Adam, right in his face and satisfied with his conquest. "I'm sitting with you, Adam."

"Sure, champ." Adam winked at Rosa.

"That was a beautiful tribute to your father, don't you think, Edgar?" she asked.

"Yes, especially the stories Uncle Lloyd and Uncle Adam told. It gave me better memories of Dad." He looked directly across to Adam. "You're going to stay with us longer, aren't you?"

Edgar is expressing endearment in calling him Uncle Adam. That's good progress.

"Your Mom and I need to talk about that. With Christmas and the service, we haven't discussed it. I guess you'll be going back to school after New Year's Day?"

"Yes, and it is okay with Will and me if you want to stay."

Adam was overwhelmed at Edgar's young sincerity, and no one spoke. All eyes were on Adam, and Rosa intercepted.

"There's so much you'll want to see in New York, Adam. I have to see about my job at Macy's, but there's plenty to take place in the next few weeks."

"I'll make sure you are taken care of, Rosa—you and the boys. We'll get through everything together."

The waitress arrived for orders and they relaxed with the distraction.

"What'll you have little man?" She asked Will.

"I'm having burger and fries please."

As the waitress jotted it, Edgar spoke up. "What's the blue plate? I saw the sign outside." Her hand covered a smirk.

"Well, young sir, it is meatloaf and mashed potatoes, but you can have fries with it if you'd rather. And mixed vegetables."

"Yes, please, but I'll take the mashed."

Rosa picked a ham steak dinner with coffee, and added milk for the boys, and Adam debated between the meatloaf and a burger and fries. He peered at both boys for a response, and made a compromise to satisfy everyone.

"I'll have meatloaf with fries."

As the waitress left, she turned around to hear Will's small voice. "I'll have mine on a blue plate too."

With little discussion, the food was devoured. Rosa declined desert and Adam insisted on ice cream sundaes for Edgar and Will, but he'd try the apple pie.

Will made his first attempt at 'Uncle'. "I'm glad you like pie, Uncle Adam; my Mom makes the best ones."

"Then tomorrow we'll bake," Rosa declared. "I have apples in the fridge. We'll get a pint of vanilla ice cream and make a feast of it."

Exhausted from the day's hugs and strangers' well-wishes, Will and Edgar didn't balk at bedtime.

Adam questioned Edgar. "Does the tooth fairy come to this house?"

"Oh yes!" Edgar dug it from his pocket and held it up. "Last year, I lost another front tooth and in the morning a whole quarter was under my pillow and my tooth was gone."

Will was eager to snitch. "We tied his tooth to the bedroom door knob and I slammed it. There was a lot of blood. It was great, Mom!"

She closed her eyes. "Next time we'll find a gentler way."

Certain the boys were asleep, Adam rifled his pockets for the shiniest quarter, and held it up for Rosa's okay. Sliding his hand under Edgar's pillow, he exchanged it with the tooth.

"It's like being Santa Claus again."

When Adam returned, Rosa had unwound on the sofa, watching Perry Como's Christmas Show on television.

With the orchestra's accompaniment, Patty Page began *The Tennessee Waltz.* Adam turned off the lights and reached for her hands, then pulled her gently to her feet in an embrace for a magical waltz, with the room in the black and white glow of the TV.

Laying her head on his shoulder, she let her body sway to the rhythm of romance and the beating of Adam's heart.

"This is a perfect night!"

24

Immigration Conundrum

Two days after the memorial, Adam told Rosa he wouldn't be by the apartment for several days this week as he had to get through some intense business. The decision was difficult for him, but they'd reached a crossroads that needed to be resolved.

"I would give you the world on a platter right now if I could. We both understand the obstacles in the next stage."

He put his arms around her and she touched his face as he kissed her. "Will and Edgar have been more accepting than I had ever imagined, and now I've fallen in love not only with their mother, but with them."

"You said we'd get through all this together," she said.

"Rosa, let me tackle my prospects in New York and see what the possibilities are. I left my affairs in Germany in my father's care, and he knows best the intricacies of immigration to a foreign country."

"I understand, Adam. Your father is a treasure indeed."

Rosa hoped her words would hide her hurt at the news of days apart.

No, I haven't taken him for granted. My love for Adam has only increased since he came to New York and I treasure every moment. I don't know if my heart can respect his decision.

"I sent the trust papers to your bank on 34th and now I only need to sign the papers and you'll have access to the fund at your pleasure. Other matters I don't want to burden you with."

Her arms tightened around his shoulders and he saw a pained look of rejection on her face, taking him back to when their feelings culminated in Heidelberg, with that longing almost too much to bear.

"Can I give the boys something to look forward to, Adam? Will you come for Sunday supper?"

"Sunday . . . that sounds so far away. Of course, I will."

Adam's first business was at the Marine Bank, to relinquish authority to Rosa for the Brand estate. After two days of transatlantic calls to Bogdan Armbruster, the accounts were in order and ready to issue the monthly checks.

Bogdan said other matters of the estate were well in hand, and added that his mother also sent love and was hopeful of his return to Heidelberg in the coming year.

His next meetings were with the U.S. Immigration Board at the Federal Plaza. Their reception was positive, that his background in law and his ability as a German translator bode him well for a preferential green card. It wasn't contingent on him marrying a U.S. citizen, although that could secure him a place and advance him in priority.

At the German Immigration office, he was referred for interviews to two competing Manhattan law firms dealing with international business. With no promise of a job, they did highlight his experience and degrees from two respected German institutions.

However the green card committee cautioned him frankly that as impressive as his case would be, there was also a backlog of other highly skilled immigration applicants seeking relocation to New York.

On her first day returning to Macy's, Rosa carried both excitement and apprehension, with so many unexpected changes since she was here last.

Her face brightened at the usual cheerful words from Harold at the elevator, and she exchanged Christmas greetings to other employees on the way to the staff room and the glove department.

"Oh Iris, I've missed you. I'm glad to be home with my family, but the fairy tale romance hasn't yet found an ending."

She mostly longed for encouragement, and laid out the long story of what had happened since her arrival in Germany, and her feelings for Adam.

"Dear Rosa, it's clear that you are madly in love with this man, and I do see that you've accepted Jake's passing." She laid her hand on Rosa's forearm.

"That's water under the bridge at this point, but thank you. It's been a whirlwind romance to be sure, but in the last few days, I feel Adam pulling away from me. Perhaps the instant family and how I have relied on him are giving him second thoughts."

"Second thoughts about what?"

"About marrying me . . . I can't bear to lose him. He's taking a sort of time out—I thought we would face our issues together."

"I can see that. Now how have the boys taken to having a new person in your life?"

"Will has such vague memories of Jake and has been able to see Adam as a father figure. Edgar was a bit suspect at first, but at the diner the other night, he told Adam it was okay for him to stay. It would break my heart to see my beautiful boys have to go through rejection."

"If he asked for time to get things in order, I believe he's displaying integrity and shows respect for you. Put yourself in his shoes. He's unsure if he is even legally allowed to stay, and any man wants to be the bread-winner and take care of his family. Have you actually talked about getting married?"

"See, I told you I need a common sense talk, Iris. I'll try to be patient and not jump to my own conclusions. I assumed that if a man gets on an airplane and follows the love of his life to a foreign country, there would be a future for them. Yet I admit he has not officially proposed."

"I'll hold you to that common sense theme, Rosa. Now here come the Clark sisters. Must be a Christmas return."

A pair of matronly women, dressed alike, approached the counter.

"I'd like to return these gloves. They came with a lipstick smudge."

Iris winked at Rosa. "Dear Edith, let me have a look. It is much like the colour of lipstick you're wearing." Iris laid them on tissue paper, and with a spray from under the counter, she gently dabbed until the stain disappeared.

"There that's better, Edith."

Iris didn't wish to embarrass the sisters, and Edith struggled momentarily to respond. As on other occasions, usually at the first of the month, she had intended to obtain a full cash refund, in her mischievous way.

Edith's counterpart, Millie, leaned in taking over the leadership of the pair. "You see girls, we're a bit short on the rent this month. Edith needs $12.50."

As long time customers, the two women had a personal relationship with Iris and Rosa, and today they were clearly flustered, caught in this awkward situation.

Rosa stepped forward. "Did I tell you ladies that I went to Germany before Christmas? While I was there, I met a wise and wonderful clockmaker that taught me about benevolence. As it turns out, I have extra benevolence. If you promise to come and buy again at Macy's glove counter, I'll be happy to chip in the $12.50 as my own belated Christmas gift."

Slipping the money into a gift envelope, she laid it on the counter in front of Edith and Millie.

Edith reached timidly for the envelope. "You are a dear girl, Rosa. I can't thank you enough. You will make some man very happy one day."

"I really hope so."

Rosa and Iris both observed the ladies' contentment as they left toward the elevator.

"Iris, I got so tied up in relationship catch-up, I forgot to mention that I received a generous inheritance from Jake's family. I can afford to do that without any hardship and it certainly felt good to see Edith's face. My affairs are well taken care of without having to work anymore."

"You're not quitting?"

"The people I work with and the regulars I see on my way are part of my life too. I'll reduce my hours so I can be home more for the boys after school, but I'd like to keep a shift or two each week."

Adam's interviews went back to back for three days, and he settled into a short term boarding house within an easy commute to the brownstone. At a Friday meeting about his green card application, he received good news of a letter from a Manhattan law firm offering a permanent position. At the German consulate, they offered a few immediate weekend hours assisting newly arrived Germans with translation.

Confident from his week's accomplishments, he had one more item of determination before Sunday night's supper. He had set Mr. Bachmann's snow globe on the night stand, and he picked it up to examine it again.

He was enjoying the big city atmosphere, and in the to and fro of meetings, he stopped at the Rockefeller Center's great Norway spruce, with its guard of white wired snowmen.

"I bet the boys haven't seen this."

He walked briskly and into the cool air he whistled the tune he'd heard Ludwig Bachmann hum so often—*Santa Claus is Coming to Town.*

25

Sunday surprise in Queens

To add to Rosa's excitement, Will and Edgar paraded constantly in front of the window for the first glimpse of him. Will was most direct with his feelings.

"Mom, why has Adam been away so long? Doesn't he like us anymore?"

"Of course he does. He's had business matters this week and needed the extra hours to work."

Will was holding a rolled up paper tied with string. "I've got a present for Uncle Adam."

"What is it, Will?"

"Have to wait, Mom; it's for Adam."

Edgar was hanging over the side of an armchair by the parlor window, and jumped up suddenly. "It's him. I see him."

The two raced to the door and Edgar landed first downstairs to greet Adam. Rosa understood, watching them expose their hearts, as she could barely wait to put her arms around her love. She deliberately hadn't done so in front of Will and Edgar, but today would be different.

Will hitched a ride halfway up the stairs, and Edgar pulled his free hand. "We found him, Mom."

Rosa stood in the doorway in Angelina's alabaster combs and a new dress. She moved closer and slid her arm through his and around his back, then rested her head on his shoulder and whispered, "I love you, Adam Armbruster."

She clung tightly, enjoying his five o'clock shadow against her face and breathing in faint traces of his aftershave. She wiped her lipstick off his cheek.

His nose sniffed towards the kitchen.

"It's pot roast. Hope you like that."

"I've come with a big appetite, and it smells fabulous. I missed you guys and I want to hear every single thing since I was gone."

"Why did you go away, Uncle Adam?" Edgar asked.

"Yeah," Will said and let go of his pent up thoughts, almost to tears. "I was 'fraid you went to Garminy and wouldn't come back for us."

Adam rumpled Will's hair. "I wouldn't go off to Germany without letting you know. I've grown attached to you."

"But you won't fight in war, will you?" Edgar prodded. "We wouldn't want you to go away and leave us."

Rosa quickly drew them back. "Will and Edgar, wash up. Supper's ready, and tell Adam about your week as we eat."

Before they even got to the table, Will started, and Edgar interrupted. Then Will again. "We tried to get the trains going good like you did, but we couldn't. We played Snakes

& Ladders with Mom and baked lots. Mrs. Fitch says to keep busy when you're sad."

Adam promised to get at the train set with them, then said a prayer of thanksgiving, holding Rosa's hand under the table.

After dinner, the eyes turned to Adam to hear of *his* plans.

"Tomorrow is New Year's Eve and I am making special plans for our family, if that's alright?"

"Like a surprise? I have a surprise for you too, Uncle Adam."

Will held out the roll of paper, glowing from ear to ear.

"For me?"

With care, Adam untied the string and unrolled it to open a crayon drawing of four people, all holding hands standing in front of a house.

"That's us, Uncle Adam."

Adam's eyes well up as he waited for his composure. "Why Will, this is the best picture I've ever had. Thanks, pal. I'm honored to be included in your family picture."

"What special plans?" Edgar prompted.

"Most of it will be a surprise, but I need the three of you to be ready at four o'clock. Dress up as it's a special occasion."

"Mom, can I wear ladyhosen?"

"It's still winter, Will. You need long pants."

"Can I . . . Uncle Adam?" Will bypassed Rosa's suggestion and his eyes were pleading for a reprieve.

"No, Will. Do as your mother says." Will sank into his chair, experiencing the first harsh word from his new idol, and tried again. "If I can't wear ladyhosen, I won't go." He peeked up for a response.

"Please, we had such a lovely dinner, let's not be sullen," Rosa cautioned. Adam and Rosa whispered, then she had an idea. "Wear your long pants in the taxi, but bring your ladyhosen and change when you're there. Adam says they'd look fine there. How's that?"

"Okey dokey!"

Alone with Adam, she explained. "I'm sorry, he's been cranky all week. He worries you'll leave and go to war. He sees you as his father replacement and fears you might die too."

"I'm not going anywhere, Rosa. Just a little more patience until tomorrow night. I should leave for the evening and give the boys space for now."

Adam rose to gather his coat without an explanation and kissed her at the door.

"I'll be seeing you soon, my love."

Adam began his work at the law office the next morning, mainly for orientation and introduction. The atmosphere was festive, with employees preparing to go home at two o'clock to celebrate New Year's Eve and the holiday.

From the skyscraper, he scurried toward 5th Avenue to an elegant façade with grand glass doors and concierge service.

Although I'm new to New York, I'm a quick learner and know that any girl would love a piece of jewelry from Tiffany's.

The store's hundred year reputation for the finest was what Adam was looking for. A meticulously coiffed man in a black suit met Adam at the door.

"Good day, Sir. May I be of assistance?" The man checked his watch.

"I suppose you're closing soon for the holiday."

"We have all the time you need, Mr . . ."

"Armbruster, Adam Armbruster."

"Are you looking for anything in particular?"

"Yes, I am. I've walked by your window several days this week and the item I wanted seems have been removed."

"We regularly change our displays. Can you describe it and I'll see if it's still available?"

Adam moved to the shining glass cases and wall shelves, glittering with diamonds and gems.

"No need. That's it, right there."

In the center of the display was a royal blue velvet tray with a diamond solitaire encircled with four smaller ones, two on each side.

"You have excellent taste, Adam."

The new confidante moved close to the case and withdrew the key, then placed the tray under brilliant lights for inspection.

Adam felt giddy with pleasure. "Yes, that's it. That's the one I want."

"You haven't asked the price, Adam."

"I know your jewelry is known to be expensive, but I want quality and assurance that my girl will like it."

"I couldn't have said it better." The gentleman pulled a card out from the box with the price tag for Adam to see.

"Will you accept an international check?"

Next, Adam walked to the Lunt-Fontanne Theater, formerly The Globe, near the corner of 15th and Broadway. He had no difficulty finding it as he could see the grand arches and regimental display of banners and headlines from down the block.

As he neared the box office, he heard the sweet sound of Edelweiss. "Yes, this is it!"

Above him, 'The Sound of Music' was a blaze of thousands of yellow lightbulbs.

At Adam's turn at the box office, the clerk scoffed that he should think that tickets might be available for that evening. "We sell out a year in advance."

The young girl softened when she saw his dejection. "Wait a minute, Sir, I'll see if there is anything at all."

To this point, everything was going according to plans, but suddenly he felt like his balloon of ecstasy was pin pricked.

The young woman returned, and he braced himself.

"This is your lucky day, Mister. The Vandenbergs just cancelled—four seats by the rail in the first balcony."

She waved four tags in the air.

"Thank you, Ma'am. I'm proposing to my new family today."

Hurrying to his boarding house, Adam mentally walked himself through the steps for the rest of the day.

"This has to be perfect!"

After a shave and change of clothes, he called for a taxi to Queens. In his navy dress coat and brown fedora, he looked dashing. At precisely four, the cab pulled up to the Flushing brownstone.

"Please wait here; I need to collect my family."

Will and Edgar were already standing on the front porch with the door open. Rosa waited for Adam to come to her.

"I'm so happy, Adam, and the boys are on tenterhooks waiting for their surprise."

"I promise not to disappoint."

The four slid over in the back seat of the full-sized sedan with the boys in the middle.

"To the Lunt- Fontanne on Broadway please."

Rosa recognized the theater name, but said nothing so the anticipation would continue for Will and Edgar.

The cab stopped directly at the doors of the grand palace.

"Ooh, this is super!" Edgar muttered.

"Yeah, Mom," Will echoed. "Super."

"We're going to see a great musical called *The Sound of Music*. It's about a singing family in the Second World War that escaped into the Alps. Although they live in Austria, it is very like Heidelberg and the Germany I grew up in."

"Will and Edgar, you'll get to see what it was like for Daddy and Uncle Adam where they grew up," Rosa said. "It's about a family that stays together no matter what."

Elegance oozed from the theater's colorful carpets at the lobby, to brass rails, and plush cushioned seats with armrests.

A young man ushered them to the first balcony and Will held tight to Adam's hand as he peered over the rail to the stage below.

"It's far, Uncle Adam. I won't fall out, will I?"

"No . . . I'll make sure."

Adam manoeuvred the seating to be next to Rosa. Will was at the end beside Adam, with Edgar inside by his mother. The boys pored over a Rodgers and Hammerstein brochure, looking at every picture over and over.

The live stage action enamored the boys, with their curiosity and imaginations expanded about everything from the stage lights and orchestra to raindrops on roses. They stayed glued to every detail, with questions about the songs *My Favorite Things*, *Do-Re-Mi* and the bedtime rendition of *So Long Farewell* by the von Trapps. At *Eidelweiss*, Will leaned to his Mom. "I know this one. It was at Dad's remembering service."

When the house lights went up for intermission, they burst into excited chatter, comparing their own lists of favorite things in their brief lives.

"Thanks, Uncle Adam," Edgar said. "It's a good surprise. Can you teach us to yodel?"

"As a matter of fact I can. My father and my grandfather yodeled, and sometime soon we'll give it a try. After the show, we'll go for dinner. Then if you're not too tired, we'll watch the big diamond ball drop in Times Square at midnight."

"Adam you have been so generous to us," Rosa said. "I'm very grateful for tonight."

At the end, they remained in their seats absorbing the finale, all applauding except Will who stopped and looked particularly sullen.

"What is it, my little man?" Rosa asked.

Addressing Adam, he started. "Did you like it when they get married and they all adopt each other?"

"Yes, I liked that very much."

It was an opening Adam couldn't resist. He cleared his throat and pulled out the Tiffany's box and turned to Rosa. She was oblivious to the exit of patrons, and her heart pounded.

He spoke first to the boys. "We have so much to celebrate at the end of an old year and the start of the new one. I was born in Germany and spent my life there up 'til now with my family. I was never blessed to have children of my own, nor a loving companion to share my whole life with.

"Rosa dearest, you are the light and love of my life and I'd be honored if you, Edgar and Will would marry me.

Everything I have I give to you, and I promise to love you more and more every day for the rest of our lives."

Will sullenly followed his mother and his eyes grew wide. "Please, Mom, please!"

Adam moved over to where Rosa was waiting, bent on one knee and opened the velvet box.

"I knew it, Uncle Adam, I knew it," Edgar said.

"I love you with all my heart and I can't bear to be another day without you. Of course, my answer is yes."

Adam stood and pulled Rosa to her feet, and in a strong embrace he kissed her for what seemed like a long time to Will and Edgar. Rosa cupped his face into her hands, and tears streamed her face.

Edgar couldn't wait. "Does this mean that Will and I are adopted?"

"Absolutely, if your mother agrees that we can be a family."

The queue moved quickly for them outside the nearby rail car diner. At the front of the line, Adam made a discreet request to the hostess for a bottle of champagne to be delivered to the table, with ginger ale for the boys.

As the waiter topped the glass flutes, Adam explained to the boys that the bubbly drinks are to celebrate the importance of today. He raised his glass, followed by Rosa and then the boys. "I'd like to make a toast to my new family."

"Yippee! Isn't this the best New Year's ever, Edgar? I knew Santa Claus was real—I asked him to bring us a new Dad. "

"Did you really think that Santa could do something like that?" Edgar whispered, out of range.

"He said it would take a little longer than for Christmas but I needed to keep hoping. What did you ask for, Edgar?"

"I asked for a whole family," Edgar confessed. "You don't suppose he really did this?"

At Times Square, they found their way to the bleacher benches, but as hard as the boys tried, they were tired from an eventful night, and Rosa and Adam fought through the crowd for a cab home. With the boys tucked in, Adam found the American Bandstand program in time for the countdown.

Drawing Rosa under the mistletoe, he held and kissed her, and she imagined their hearts beating together. Adam lingered, at the scent of rose cologne and lavender shampoo, and he noticed the alabaster combs.

"I'll love you forever, Rosa Stanford. I'd like to marry you as soon as possible."

26

December 1963, Heidelberg One Year Later

Rosa was midway through her pregnancy when they returned to Heidelberg for the Christmas holidays. It had been a year since Adam had seen his parents and brother, and the matchmaker, Ludwig Bachmann.

As the plane rose over Manhattan, the wings tilted in a salute to the miniaturized skyscrapers, the Hudson River and Statue of Liberty. The boys were seated in the two seats in front of them, and Rosa pointed over the seat, smirking at the two faces crammed to the window.

"The boys have become so fascinated by this adventure, almost in disbelief. Look at their eyes examining the scenery." She laughed out loud. "And we've actually convinced Will that it is Germany instead of Garminy."

Rosa watched out her own window hoping she might see Queens, but it was long gone. "I love living in New York, but I also can't wait to see our German family again."

"You know my parents ask about you in every letter. We should be prepared that they'll brag and parade the boys to their friends. At last they have grandchildren to pamper.

"Last week I wrote to Mr. Bachmann to make sure St. Nicolas finds Will and Edgar this year at my parents' house. I promised we'll come for a visit. The boys should see the secret workshop."

"Yes . . . my dear clockmaker," Rosa sighed. "No Christmas can now be complete without him."

With the time change, morning came too early for the groggy boys, and they again jammed together at the window to watch the sunrise. On the approach to Frankfurt, they flew low over Heidelberg, and Rosa shivered at the sight of the castle and bridge, and the distant Neckar River.

"From Frankfurt, we'll take the train instead of a car," Adam said." It'll be another thrill for our train-crazy boys."

At Adam's parents' house, a handmade banner draped over the entrance—'Wilkommen Adam Rosa Edgar Will'. A few family friends were at the house for the welcome, and everyone flocked outside to their taxi, with a commotion of hugs and kisses that the boys had never seen before.

"I've reserved a family dinner tonight," Adam said. "It's at the Spengel's. I'll call Mr. Bachmann too; he should join us."

Will went straight to the oompah band stage, where he stood close to the tuba player, pretending to be in the band. Edgar abandoned him right away to return to the table.

Adam called Will back, and the three of them crouched together to see where he had etched his name as a boy.

As they snickered, Mrs. Spengel stood over them. At the sight of her, they tightened up their faces of mischief. Her hands were on her hips.

"So perhaps we should add another generation of Armbruster to our décor," she said, handing a marker to Edgar.

Hesitating, he watched her eyes longer for confirmation. Then with a glance to Adam, he carefully printed 'Edgar Stanford Armbruster'. Beside it, Will used large block letters, but only his first name.

Ludwig Bachmann was the last to arrive. Jolly as they remembered and keen to see his friends, he bounded across the room to the table, leaving no doubt who he was going to see.

Will nudged Edgar. "That's him, I'm sure—that's Santa from the Macy's store."

Long after dusk, Rosa peered into the window of the clock store.

"Adam, I see a glow from the back and I know they're in here. Tomorrow, can we go up to Abel's house? I've thought about it for a year and I want to know if the jingling and singing still happens below. It's a magical opportunity for the boys."

"And for you," he teased. "But we'll go tonight after Church and hope the red cloaked man shows himself.

"I adore you for letting me believe too. I wish you had been with me on the roof that night . . . It was like a veil of magical stardust gently fell on me."

After Church, they all walked to the clockmaker's shop and the new Brand Museum. In front under a lamp post, Adam took Rosa in his arms.

"I was standing right here the moment I knew I had to have you. That's when the snow globe appeared in my pocket."

The dim lamps in the stairwell were still on until late for the tenants, but nonetheless it felt eerie.

Halfway up the stairs, Rosa put her hand up, then a finger to her lips for the boys to stop and listen. Focused on far off sounds, she heard gentle jingling and cheery voices.

"Does anyone else hear that?"

"I hear noises, Mom," Edgar whispered on the brink of his imagination.

Adam urged them up to Abel's apartment and unlocked the door. For the Christmas season, it had been fully decorated, with a magnificent Christmas tree, in the place it had been in the old photos.

He plugged in the lights and turned on the lamps. Rosa had goosebumps as they stood magically in the scene that Abel's family would have cherished, that Jake and Adam knew as boys.

Edgar's eyes widened round. "Dad, is this the house where Father Christmas came when you were little like us?

"Yes . . . and when I was your age, I used to go to a special spot in the back bedroom. That's where I slept when I had a sleepover at Granddad's. I'll show you."

Lying on the floor, Adam rolled under the cot by the window. Flat on his belly, he said, "You won't see anything standing there, boys. Join me to have a look."

The three were side by side on their stomachs when Adam pulled up from the floorboards a black metal heating grate, an old-fashioned, heavy ornate wrought-iron type.

"Be quiet and still, then squint your eyes like a pirate so you can see through this peep hole I made once."

Edgar was the first to see it, then Will. Gasps of delight came from under the bed, then wiggling to be the first to tell Rosa.

"Mom, it's Santa's workshop, it really is," Edgar said. "The elves are making toys and clocks, and they're all wearing lederhosen."

Will was almost hysterical, still peering through the grate. "Look, Dad, see down there . . . that's Santa."

The sounds of their gasps of wonderment drew the jovial figure's attention, and as he looked up, the workshop hushed and the music and jingling muted.

"Gee, Dad, we scared him away," Will pined in disappointment they'd been found out.

By the tree in the parlor, Rosa consoled them with her soft words at the event. "This was awesome. Christmas is in the heart, boys, and you must always believe . . ."

She stopped to listen to soft jingling again, then it grew louder, with heavy footsteps on the stairs.

"Ho-ho-ho!"

"The door," Edward and Will shouted and froze in awe. They looked to Rosa, then to Adam to get the door. Their mouths all opened in disbelief.

"So it *is* the red cloak from the clockmaker's shop," Rosa whispered to herself.

From the entrance, Father Christmas said, "I heard there were boys here on my Nice list. May I come in?"

With large strides into the parlor, the jolly man settled into Abel Brand's armchair, and called the boys to his lap.

His laughter filled the room, and Edgar climbed up first.

"Well, Edgar Stanford Armbruster, what special thing would you like for Christmas?" Edgar whispered close into the old man's ear.

"And William Stanford Armbruster, what's your wish this year?"

"I have everything I want. But I wish for a train set and a dad for another boy whose dad got lost in the war."

Will peered closer and tugged gently on the beard.

"Mom, it *is* Santa. He's the same one from Macy's."

THE END

If you enjoyed Clockmaker's Christmas, you might like the many short chronicles in my 620 page historical fiction.

HOMAGE: CHRONICLES OF A HABITANT
A ten generation historical fiction, in a series of short chronological stories, beginning in France in the 1600s. A 500 year journey based on a family's lives, tragedies and immigration to North America. Experience typical life as the early migrants travel from France to settle in Quebec, with generational conflicts and cultural clashes in the founding of the new land.

Shirley Burton

shirleyburtonbooks.com